MOUNTAIN DOG

MARGARITA ENGLE

MOUNTAIN DOG

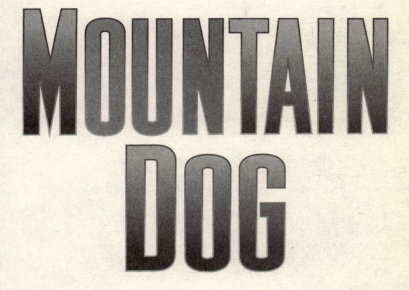

ILLUSTRATIONS BY
OLGA & ALEKSEY IVANOV

 SQUARE FISH 🐾 HENRY HOLT AND COMPANY 🐾 NEW YORK

SQUARE FISH

An Imprint of Macmillan
175 Fifth Avenue
New York, NY 10010
mackids.com

Square Fish books may be purchased for business or promotional use. For information
on bulk purchases, please contact the Macmillan Corporate and Premium Sales
Department at (800) 221-7945 x5442 or by e-mail at specialmarkets@macmillan.com.

Library of Congress Cataloging-in-Publication Data
Engle, Margarita.
Mountain dog / Margarita Engle ; illustrations by Olga and Aleksey Ivanov.
pages   cm
ISBN 978-1-250-04424-2 (paperback) / ISBN 978-0-8050-9893-8 (e-book)
[1. Novels in verse.   2. Rescue dogs—Fiction.   3. Dogs—Fiction.   4. Human-
animal relationships—Fiction.   5. Great-uncles—Fiction.   6. Foster home
care—Fiction.   7. Hispanic Americans—Fiction.   8. Sierra Nevada (Calif. and
Nev.)—Fiction.]   I. Ivanov, O. (Olga), illustrator.   II. Ivanov, A. (Aleksey),
illustrator.   III. Title.
PZ7.5.E54Mo 2013   [Fic]—dc23   2012027680

Originally published in the United States by Henry Holt and Company
First Square Fish Edition: 2014
Book designed by April Ward
Square Fish logo designed by Filomena Tuosto

10 9 8 7 6 5 4

AR: 5.9 / LEXILE: 1050L

For Curtis and the dogs,
with love and gratitude
——M. E.

To Misha, a great mountain dog,
who helped our son to find his path
——O. I. and A. I.

MOUNTAIN DOG

FIDE CANEM (TRUST THE DOG)
—Ancient Roman search-and-rescue proverb

THAT OTHERS MAY LIVE
—Official motto of search-and-rescue

teams all over the world

TONY THE BOY
NO NO NO MAYBE

In my other life there were pit bulls.
The puppies weren't born vicious,
but Mom taught them how to bite,
turning meanness into money,
until she got caught.

Now I don't know where I'll live,
or what sort of foster family
I'll have to face each morning.
I dread the thought of a new school,
new friends, no friends, no hope. . . .
No! No no no no no.

But the social-worker lady doesn't listen
to NO. She's like a curious puppy, running,

exploring, refusing to accept collars and fences.
She keeps promising to find a relative who will
give me a place where I can belong.

I don't believe her.
There aren't any relatives—
not any that I've ever met.
I know I'm right, but family court
makes me feel dumb, with judges
and uniforms
wrapped up in rules.
It's a world made for grown-ups,
not unlucky kids.

Even the angriest pit bulls
are friendlier than my future.

Everyone talks about dog years,
but all I can see now is minutes.
Each impossibly long dog minute
with the frowning judge
and cheerful social worker
feels like it could go on and on
forever.

Mom's cruelty to animals
was her fault, not mine, but now
I'm the one suffering, as if her crimes
are being blamed on me.

When the social worker keeps smiling,
I find it hard to believe she's actually found
a relative, a great-uncle, Tío Leonilo.
What a stupid name!
Maybe I can call him Leo the Lion,
or just *tío*, just uncle, as if I actually
know my mother's first language,
the Spanish she left behind
when she floated away
from her native island
with me in her mean belly.

The social worker promises me
that although Tío is old—nearly fifty—
he's cool.

He lives on a mountain, rescues lost hikers,
guides nature walks, and takes care
of trees. He's a forest ranger.

She might as well say he's a magician
or a genie who lives in a bottle.

I've spent all my life in the city.
All I know is Los Angeles noise, smog,
buses, traffic, and the gangs, and my mom,
the dogs, fangs, blood, claws.

Nothing makes sense.
Why would a cool uncle want to share
his long-lost relative's kid-trouble?
This can't be real.
Real life should feel real,
but this feels all weird and scary,
like a movie with zombies or aliens.

When a man in a forest green uniform
walks into the courtroom, he hugs me
and calls me Tonio, even though Mom
never called me anything but Tony
or Hey You or Toe Knee. . . .

Out in the hall, Tío shows me a photo
of a dog, a chocolate Lab—goofy grin,

silly drool—not a fighting dog,
just a friendly dog, eager, a pal.

Tío walks me out of that crazy
scary courthouse, into a parking lot
where the happy dog is waiting
in a forest green truck.
I have to meet Gabe's welcoming
doggie eyes and sniffy nose,
even though I'm not ready to meet
nice dogs, cool uncles, or anyone else.

Well, maybe just one sniff is okay.
When I pat Gabe on his soft, furry head,
he gives my hand a few trusting,
slobbery licks.
Yuck.

2 GABE THE DOG
YES YES YES ALWAYS

The boy sees how I sniff, and he breathes too, smelling the deep odors of night and bright fragrance of day. Time is all mixed together in one long, endless pleasure of sniffing. We open our noses, inhaling everything—all we need is in the air.

I love the sound of his boy voice. Tonio. Tony. Not a very hard name to remember. I love the smell of his hands. The finger scent rhymes with good smells, food smells, friendly smells. Only his shoes hold an unfriendly odor. Bad dogs have walked near him. Strange dogs. Dangerous dogs. Their stench rhymes with bear scent and lion scent and the stink of rough places where stray dogs are caged.

The boy moves his head in slow circles, eyes closed,
   nose open.

The truck roars up our mountain. Aromas rush in. We
   lift our noses

together, pushing our heads out the wide-open window

into a wild place

where only scent

matters.

We sniff.

We share the road,

the window,

and clear

invisible

air!

We will always be friends.

Always.

3 TONY THE BOY
SCENT TRAILS

I've slept in plenty of ugly
splintered
stinky
spiderwebby
nightmarish
hard
wooden
doghouses.

This place is different,
even though it's not a real
house, just a two-room cabin,
with one whole room
for me.

The knotty pine walls
are filled with pictures of trees
and animals—no family photos, no
pictures of Mom when she was little.
I wonder what she was like.
Was she already fierce, or did she
look shy and scared
like me?

Tío's brown dog claims my bed,
dropping his weight over my ankles,
as if to keep me from sprinting
away
in my dreams. . . .

Life is so weird. Gabe is a happy,
almost-as-smart-as-any-human
creature, while I feel like a worn-out
zoo beast.

I lie awake for a long time,
gazing out the cabin window at stars
that seem to be cradled by branches.

Our drive up the mountain
was so long and dizzying
that I can't even begin to imagine
how far away
from my other life
I am now.

When I finally sleep, I dream
of a funny future. No fangs
or claws. Just me and Gabe,
only he's a serious human,
and I'm the playful pup.

Then it's morning, and Gabe
starts begging to go outside,
but when I glance out the window,
my view of a forest is so unfamiliar
that I stay where I am, motionless
and silent.

Pretty soon, my uncle is up
and breakfast is ready, the morning
already a flurry of surprises.
No one has ever cooked for me.
Not once. Oatmeal might not be

my favorite, but today it tastes
warm and comforting.

Tío says his cabin is so remote,
so high in the Sierra Nevadas,
that I'll have to go to an old-style
three-room mountain school—
grades six through eight together
in one class. I'll be with big kids,
and even though I'm tall, I'm only eleven
and a half. How am I going to survive
around twelve and thirteen-year-olds?

The worst part of picturing myself
at a new school is those moments
at the board, showing everyone
that I can't ever
do any
of the math.

I'm nervous around fractions
and percentages, but word problems
about money are the ones
that really terrify me.

The social worker says it's because
at home, when I showed that I knew
how to count, Mom made me keep track
of greedy bets
at the growling, snarling,
bloodthirsty dogfights.
So instead of practicing numbers,
I just learned letters, and then
I figured out how to keep my words
to myself.

Now, right after breakfast, Tío invites me
to help him take Gabe for a rambling walk
in the woods, where wild pine trees
smell like Christmas, even though
it's springtime.

The forest is shadowy green,
with spiky red flowers sprouting
from bright patches of snow.
My first snow.
My first mountain.
My first off-leash dog.
No chain.

No muzzle.
No scars
or scabs.

Gabe follows a scent, nose to the ground,
nose in the air, back and forth, tracing
a pattern as he follows a smell
toward its source.

He's so thrilled that I soon share
his excitement, racing to catch a sniff
and a glimpse
of the deer or squirrel
that left this mysterious trail
of drifting air.
I wish my stupid human nose
understood all the invisible clues
that Gabe can follow! Dogs inhale
the scents of sweat, breath, skin,
poop, and pee, but they can smell
emotions, too—anger, sadness, fear,
happiness, love, hope. . . .
Dogs can even smell a tricky lie
or the soothing truth.

Gabe bounces along the trail
of mystery scent, leading me
from a scared-of-life mood
to one that feels
like music.

Tío runs and laughs with us,
but the next day, on our morning walk,
when I sit on a tree stump to rest,
he suddenly turns serious,
reassuring me that he really is
Mom's uncle—my great-uncle—
a true relative. He says he cares
what happens to me.
He tells me what happened to him.
He came to this country on a raft,
just like Mom, but years earlier,
when she was still a child.

His raft drifted, then washed ashore
and crashed on rocks, leaving him alone
and stranded on a tiny, nameless isle
for weeks, a castaway, marooned,
just like Robinson Crusoe.

He had to learn how to survive
by eating seaweed, drinking rain,
and breathing hope. . . .

I wonder if he remembers my mother
when she was tiny. I hope she was gentle,
sweet, and kind. I hope she loved animals,
and liked everybody,
and was too young to know
that life can be dangerous.
All I know about her is that
after growing up and floating away
from her island, she reached a rough city
where she met mean people
who used drugs and dogfights
as cruel ways to make money.

Tío swears that if he'd known
where she was, he would have tried
to help her, he would have struggled
to help me.

When he's finished talking,
I shake off the tears, and he asks
if I want to sing.

That makes me grin, but he's not joking,
so we pile into the truck with Gabe,
and we whirl around mountain curves,
until the steep road ends at a jumble
of barns and corrals
beyond a crooked wooden sign
that announces
   COWBOY CHURCH
   DOGS & HORSES WELCOME

I've never been to any church at all before,
and I've certainly never imagined a God
who likes horses and dogs.

Gabe treats the place like a feast
of scent, sniffing boots, jeans, hoofs,
and manure. Even the yucky smells
make him smile. He turns out to be
the kind of dog that loves to laugh
and howl.

When the cowboys and forest rangers
start to sing, Gabe joins in, off-key,
and everyone ends up chuckling,
especially me. I never thought
I could have so much fun
so soon after trading
my tough-pit-bull
real life
for this temporary
foster home
in a wild forest
that somehow feels
so much more gentle
than the city.

4 GABE THE DOG
WORD SMELLS

After horse smells and howling, we run, race, leap, noses open, eyes open, mouths open, until the floaty aroma of a passing hawk almost disappears.

Low flying. Foresty. Swoop. Chase. Hunt. Hawks leave winged trails of hunger in midair.

Snow. We're tired. We flop, dance, flap, flutter, flip. We make shapes in the softness. Tony's patterns of snow are four limbed, just like mine when I roll from side to side. Only my shape is bigger and more wispy, because it has a tail.

Snow angels. I love it when the boy shouts words with cold, clear meanings that I can smell and taste!

I twitch my nostrils, inhale deeply, swallow meanings. I make the sound, smell, and taste of each new word my own, filling my hunger for friendship. I breathe the bumpy surface of words that rhyme with the scent of humans, the aroma of happiness.

5 TONY THE BOY TRAIL ANGELS

I'm afraid to sleep, terrified
that the same old nightmares
of fangs
and claws
will keep coming back . . .

but beside me, Gabe woofs,
then drifts

into a running-dog
dream

that leads my tired mind
toward a race

where I am four legged
and fast

so swift that I can
almost
fly!

It's not a real dream,
just a half-awake
fantasy,
but it helps me feel
safe enough
to doze.

In the morning, I wonder
why people always assume that dogs
just want food. Walks are the reward
they really crave—movement,
adventure, new smells.

So I get up and take Gabe out
to sniff the forest while I wish
for a way to avoid my first day
at a new school, and a way

to visit Mom without seeing her
in a prison uniform.

An hour later, my wishing ends.
Small yellow school bus.
Tiny, splintered-wood school.
So how come it seems like a ton
of huge, scary faces?

The old-fashioned building
is plopped in a rocky patch
of flowers that smell like wildness.
Right away, a loud girl shouts
that she saw me at Cowboy Church.
Good dog, she yells, and even though
I know she must mean Gabe,
I feel strangely praised.

Mom knew what she was doing
when she trained me to obey.
So I tell myself to concentrate
on this new-school reality.
My future. My torment.
Which boy will be the first

to trip me? Which girls
can't wait to laugh?

I avoid eye contact.
If there are bullies here,
they'll take a bold gaze
as a challenge.

I've been through it so many times
that I have a reputation for battles,
even though fighting
is the last thing
I've ever
wanted
to do.

The teacher is old and friendly.
The students are young and curious.
I don't even try to learn names.
Why bother? As soon as Mom gets out
of prison, I'll have to move back
to my pit-bull life, the place
where I've always felt
muzzled
and caged.

By the end of that first long day,
all the kids know that I live
with my uncle, who has a search-
and-rescue dog. The loud girl
doesn't keep secrets.
She claims she's a reporter
for the school paper.
She wants me to join her staff,
get a press pass, help her write
stories about four-footed
trail angels.

I don't know what she means.
Are trail angels like snow angels?
Do people lie down and wave
their arms and legs
in mud or dust?

That night, when Tío asks me
about my first day of school, I don't
say much, so he takes me outdoors
in the darkness
to stargaze.

Without any traffic or streetlights,
the forest seems ancient.
I feel like a time traveler
in a distant land
where I don't know
the language
of star shapes.
Constellations.
Pictures in the sky.
Myths. Stories. Directions.
A way to find north or south
by following a path
made of light years.

Soon, the night-gazing spell is broken.
In bed, beside Gabe, ferocious dreams
grab me and shake me, biting, piercing,
spilling blood. By morning,
I feel wounded
instead of restful.

Gabe nuzzles my face, but I can't tell
if he's really trying to comfort me,

or does he just wish he could somehow
understand humans?

The next school day is oddly awkward
and friendly at the same time.
The loud girl is nosy, asking questions,
demanding answers: Who am I, where
do I come from? Am I Latino? Am I legal?
Do I like to write?
Essays? Stories? Poems?
I fall quiet. I plan to keep the answers
to myself. I haven't had to fight
at this school. My only battle
is against
my own past.

So far, there are no gangster bullies
with knives or guns. Just the nosy girl's
bossy voice. Her name is Gracie,
and she knows everyone.
She talks to other kids about me,
and she chatters to me about them.
Pretty soon, I'll probably end up

with all their names stuck in my mind,
even though I don't want to remember
anything that I'll soon have to try
to forget.

The dizzy mountain bus ride
back to Tío's cabin feels endless.
Three more days until the weekend.
All I have to do is avoid Gracie
and nosiness
and friendliness
and math.

Nightmares come and go.
Should I tell Tío? Would he know
how to stop them? Would he care?
What if he just lets me stay here
because he has to? Is there a law
that says great-uncles have to help
their relatives' kids?

By the time Saturday arrives,
sun and warmth have melted

most of the snow. Tío invites me
to climb into the truck
and go exploring with Gabe.

We glide up to high slopes,
to a snow-patched campground
where ragged hikers lounge,
leaning on grubby backpacks.

There's a trading post, with corrals
for pack animals—horses, mules,
and even a few long-necked llamas,
strange, woolly creatures
that make the day seem
like a daydreamed
adventure.

Suddenly, my other life—
my pit-bull life—starts to feel
unreal.

Catching Gabe's excitement,
I push uneasy thoughts of the past

as far away as I can. This is real.
The llamas, the wildness, the peaks.

All I want is a chance to pay attention.
Giant burgers sizzling on a campfire.
Hikers chatting in foreign languages.
The camp is a rest stop for trekkers
from all over the world: Iceland,
Australia, France, Japan.

Tío explains that people who walk
all the way from Mexico to Canada
on the Pacific Crest Trail
are called thru-hikers. The trail
is 2,650 miles long and passes through
unimaginably rugged
wilderness.

In some parts, there's no water.
In others, no warmth.

Hikers talk to me in broken English
about all the mountains they've seen,
the Alps, the Andes, the Himalayas.

I listen in wonder, trying to imagine
the size of the world.

No wonder I feel
so small.

Wild words are added
to my vocabulary when Tío gives me
my first wilderness tour.

Trail angels—the phrase Gracie used—
turn out to be dedicated professionals
like Tío, who works for free on weekends
and evenings, as a volunteer,
along with other people
whose jobs have nothing to do
with the wilderness. They just
volunteer because they love to help
by stocking food and water in caches—
bear-proof cans placed on remote paths,
just in case a weary thru-hiker
runs low on supplies, and suffers
from hunger or thirst.

Help from a stranger is called trail magic.
Food. Water. Rescue.

There are trail names, too, brave names
chosen by hikers. Explorer, Sky Walker,
Wolf Man. All the thru-hikers I meet
have trail names that sound
adventurous.

My wilderness tour
is both scary and exciting.
Sheer cliffs, tumbled boulders,
the singing
sighing
wind.

Gazing around, I imagine
how lonely it would feel
to stray from the trail
and get lost way out here,
just waiting for Tío
and a search dog
like Gabe. . . .

No wonder the hikers
call my uncle's friendly dog
a four-footed trail angel.

That night, next to Gabe,
I listen to his slow breath,
with its peaceful rhythm
like soothing music.
No nightmares.
Just sleep.

In the morning, when Gabe stares
into my eyes, I feel like I can see
his dog thoughts, his memories. . . .

Before he was adopted by Tío,
he was a stray, lost and lonely,
but now he finds lost people,
saving their lives.

Some things in life actually do
make sense.

So why can't I understand Mom?
The pit-bull fights were like
horror movies.

I didn't know how to make
the pain stop.
No wonder I have mean dreams.
Scary men. Scary dogs. I was the one
who had to patch wounds
and touch scars.

I was also in charge of the money,
the numbers, the bets.
That's why I still think of math
as a battle.

Now, when Gabe grins
and wags his tail, I feel like he's
inviting me to leave the past far behind
and play dog games—tag, tug-of-war,
victory dance!

Then it's time for Cowboy Church,
a swirl of people, horses, dogs,

all howling through songs
and prayers.

Loud Gracie trots up to me
on a spotted mare. She smiles
and waves from the height
of her perch on the horse.

By now I know that her parents
are away for a year, studying
elephants in India. So she lives
with her grandma, a retired
wildlife biologist she calls B.B.
because B.B. studies black bears
and is beautifully brave.

In a shy, quiet way
that catches me by surprise,
Gracie asks if I've checked out
the school's online newspaper.

I haven't, and I don't plan to.
I don't want to hear Gracie's
gossip.

But later, back at the cabin,
curiosity grips me.
I borrow Tío's laptop.
There it is: My name
in a story about city kids
who have to adjust to small
mountain schools.

Gracie's casually written words
make it sound so easy, but that's
because she doesn't know

that in a couple
of hours

I'll be heading
downhill

down
down
down

to the flatlands
to the visiting room
to the loneliness

of Valley State
Prison for Women.

6 GABE THE DOG
ROUNDNESS

Togetherness in the truck, on the way back from a flat place with high fences and sadness. Tony is quiet. Is he dreaming again? Is he wishing? Why does he act so lost in aloneness? I'm here. Right here. Does the boy know how much I love to study him? I watch his eyes, listen to his voice, smell his shoes, follow his hands with my nose. I need to understand this boy-silence!

Leo is the first to speak. He notices how I stare at the boy, and he calls me a professor of human behavior. He says I could teach other dogs. This gets Tony's attention. Teach *me*, the boy thinks, leaning close to press my ear with his nose as he tries to sniff my dog thoughts. Teach *me*, Tony begs with his silent-sad scent.

Show *me* how to understand a prisoner-Mom who
refuses to come into the visiting room, even though
she knows her own son is waiting there with an eager
social worker, waiting, waiting, waiting. . . .

Teach *me*, Tony's scent pleads, but I can't. There's a
human strangeness, a mystery that I don't know how
to inhale.

At twilight, on the way back uphill, we stop at a little
park. The grass is dry and weedy, but everything smells
delicious, like a name that rhymes with good or food.

Leo tosses a ball for me to chase! I show Tony how to
smell, taste, hear, see, and touch the ball's rhyming,
rolling, racing roundness. Chasing a ball right beside
me, how can Tony still feel that human aloneness? He
doesn't! He understands this togetherness chase-game.
He quickly learns to share my hunger for roundness!

Spherical objects dazzle me. Tennis balls, oranges,
apples, even my water bowl—any roundness will do.
Roll, bounce, squeak!

If I could chase the moon across the sky, I would,

but every time I try, it flies too far,
so I point my nose

and sing.

Watch out, moon!

7
TONY THE BOY
INVISIBLE CLUES

The visiting room at the prison
looked like a cafeteria, but to reach it
I had to pass through metal detectors
and a massive
scary
sliding
snap-shut
gate.

Mom left me waiting there
with Leo and the social worker.
Waiting, waiting, waiting.
Like waiting in a nightmare.
So I looked around for something

good to remember. Anything
good. Just a glimpse.

All I saw was women
in blue uniforms, mostly young,
some with tattoos on their arms
and faces, playing board games
with quiet little kids
and sad-looking grandmas.

It looked almost normal,
except for the silence
of the children.

So I had to peer farther
for something worthy of memory.
I gazed out a window and found
a view of a green lawn.
Clusters of women in blue
walked in big circles,
while others kneeled
or stood
with open mouths,
singing.

A few waved sticks of incense.
Others had scarves on their heads.
The social worker pointed out
different groups—Catholics, Hindus,
Protestants, Muslims. . . . Prison,
she said, is open to all.

I wondered what crimes
the women had committed
and how long it had taken
before they started wanting
to sing.

Mom never showed up,
so I asked to leave, and now,
on the way back uphill, after
the park, after a ball-chasing,
moon-howling, hilarious
moment of relief with Gabe,
I start to hope there might be
enough funny memories
to balance

the sad

mad

abandoned
ones.

The note Mom sent
to the social worker said
she wanted to watch a movie
in the recreation room.
She even named the actor she
couldn't stand to miss.
I like movies too, but I'd rather
have a family.

The social worker tried to be
cheerful, but Tío was realistic.
He told me he was furious.
He said Mom must be ashamed
to let me see her in prison.

He also said the real shame
was her worrying about her image
instead of my feelings.

Now, halfway up the mountain,
his phone rings, so he pulls over
and listens, nodding, agreeing
to show up right away. . . .

Pretty soon we're headed
to a search in the foothills,
a real-live mystery search
for a missing girl only three
tiny years old—she's
the daughter of migrant
farm workers, and she
wandered away from
an apple orchard,
and now
it's nighttime,
and she's still lost.
Her little dog is gone too.

Maybe they went exploring
together.

If Tío and Gabe can't
find her . . .

Well, I don't even want
to think about it.

So we drive to a farm
where volunteers gather
around a sheriff, listening
to instructions.

Tío tells me to stay close,
then introduces me to a woman
around his age. She has a nice smile,
and I can tell that my uncle
really likes her.

But she turns out to be
loud Gracie's grandma,
the bear-behavior specialist
who has a reputation
for courage.

Gracie is right beside her, just as jumpy
and exuberant as Gabe. I don't want to stay
at the sheriff's command-post table,
even though Gracie calls it base camp,

as if we're getting ready to climb
the world's tallest mountain.

I need to get away.
I want to be out *there*, searching
with Tío and his hero-dog, moving
through the whispery spring leaves,
where instead of ripe red fruit
on the trees there are just
moon white
apple flowers
glowing.

With a silvery bell on his collar
and Halloween light sticks
fitted into tabs on his bright
orange vest, Gabe sounds
like Christmas and looks
like a shooting star

as he streaks
        through the darkness
                    of night
making light
    seem like something alive
and growing. . . .

There are horsemen, too,
and horsewomen, a mounted posse
like the ones in old cowboy movies,
and modern people driving ATVs,
all-terrain vehicles that resemble
slow golf carts but zip and dart
like speeding dirt bikes.

Teams of searchers head out
in every direction.

Ground pounders! a loud voice
proclaims. Gracie. Trumpeting.
Knowing it all. Explaining.

If I wasn't so eager to understand
absolutely everything about this urgent
search for a lost kid,
I'd ignore her noisy voice,
but Gracie flashes her press pass—
Great story! she booms.
Great headline!

Soon I've learned that ground pounders
are volunteers who search on foot
without dogs, horses, or vehicles,
just headlamps, flashlights,
and their voices, shouting
the little girl's name
as they go,
until they vanish
beyond streaks of moonlight.

I know I'm supposed to stay close
to Gracie's grandma, but Gabe

is out there, leading Tío
under gnarled trees
with twisted branches
that look like natural statues
of beasts.

I'm not afraid to solve
this kind of eerie problem.
It's not math or meanness.
It's a mystery, and I need to help,
so when Gracie and B.B. are looking
the other way, I sneak
away
quietly
creeping
silently
wondering
how terrible
my punishment
will be, once my uncle
finally realizes
that I've disobeyed.

By the time Tío notices
that I'm right beside him,

he's as focused as a laser beam,
following Gabe, who races ahead
sniffing
       in a zigzag pattern
solving
       the mystery
searching for invisible
scent clues.

Gabe leads us beyond apple trees
to huge oaks, where an owl hoots
in shivery air, and my drumbeat heart
pounds with hope!

Movement. A silhouette.
Growling sounds. Fox? Coyote?
Bobcat? No! It's a dog, tiny
and white, fuzzy but tough
as it lunges and yaps at Gabe.

The little girl's pup stands his ground,
defending, protecting. He's a brave,
rabbit-size guard dog,
and close behind him, the girl
is half-hidden by a droopy branch,

her round face radiant
in moonlight.

Tío wakes her, talks to her,
checks her for injuries, then calls
the sheriff on his two-way radio,
to report the good news.
Somehow, at the exact same time,
he manages to throw a ball for Gabe
and reward him with praise
delivered in a high, squeaky voice
that sounds like pure excitement.
Hugging her dog, the girl looks
so calm that I wonder if she knew
she was lost.

I can imagine how she feels.
I used to wander all over the city,
following loyal puppies wherever
they roamed.

Back at base camp, the toddler's parents
cry and hug her, then they hug me,
and Gabe and Tío, and especially
the fuzzy pup.

I love you, the mother tells me
in two languages. *Te quiero.* Spanish.
A sad-happy sound that I haven't heard
since I was little, when Mom wasn't
quite so completely
lost.

8 GABE THE DOG
HIDE-AND-SEEK

The tiny girl's scent rhymes with home. Before the woods, back in the apple place, I could already follow her aroma of home rhyme. There is a skin smell, and baby sweat, soap, pillow, blanket, milk from her breath, and a baking-swirl of floating kitchen scents, fluffy cake made with stirred streaks of sugar, flour, salt, butter, and orchids—wild orchids—dry vanilla pods from some faraway forest.

There's the metal and fuel smell of the oven that baked the cake, and the fragrance of safety the girl felt while she was eating, before she followed her dog past the apple place to hide.

Her feet smell like orchard, but her hands are pure puppy, and she isn't afraid, not even when Leo, my wonderful Leo, changes his voice from ordinary to play-with-me!

It's that yipping, playful-workful, wild-pack-of-dogs-hunting voice that I love most of all, even more than chasing roundness, or sniffing old apple scraps on the orchard floor. It's the voice that makes me forget to keep wondering why my Leo couldn't find the girl's scent trail himself. I don't understand human noses.

9 TONY THE BOY FENCES

The quiet woods come alive
at midnight. On our way back
to the cabin, with the windows
of the truck wide open,
Gabe sniffs wild-animal smells
in the breeze. I catch a glimpse
of a deer, and there are cries
from owls
and coyotes,
and smaller noises, too,
a buzz of insects, the clang
of bullfrogs.

A black bear glides across the road,
framed by the glow of our headlights.

My uncle smiles and says he knows
this particular bear
because it's a friend
of Gracie's beautiful
grandma.

Tío is a mystery. Will I ever
understand him? Does he want
to talk about B.B.? Is he in love?

The bear passes as swiftly
as one of Mom's worst moods.
Will everything always feel
so dangerous?

Later, in the cabin, my uncle
talks to me about sneaking out to join
the search. Volunteers have to be
eighteen and expertly trained,
tested and certified by county,
state, and federal agencies.
Risk. Insurance. Liability.
Responsibility.

Tío's stern lecture sounds
like a spelling list.
All I want to think about
is Gabe's heroic triumph,
the little girl's safety,
and her tiny dog's
loyalty.

I could make up my own
spelling test, put all the words
in one sentence: Canine trail angels
are intelligent, courageous,
amazing, magical . . .
but tough pit bulls and rough moms
can be ominous, unpredictable,
perilous,
and painful.

I accept my uncle's scolding in silence,
because I know I broke a big rule,
and Tío is still talking, explaining
that he needs to trust me.

When he's finished, he adds,
Do you have any questions, *mi'jo*,
anything at all?

Mi'jo. Mi hijo. My son. My uncle
just called me son! Yes, I have lots
of questions, but the only one I suddenly
need to ask right away
is about the fighting dogs. Their safety
is my question. Those puppies were like
brothers to me. What happened to them
when Mom went to prison
and I came here?

Have they been adopted?
Do they have good homes
with patient foster parents
like Tío?

My uncle looks troubled.
He admits that the toughest dogs
might never find homes, but he also
assures me that the others
are safe now.

Safe now.
Safe.

My echoing mind almost misses
the chance to ask one more
big question: Why does B.B. study
scary bears? How did she learn
to be so beautifully
brave?

The answer is a surprise.
Tío explains that Gracie's grandma
was attacked a long time ago,
when she stepped in between
a mother bear and a cub.
The scars healed, so now she talks
to campers about bears, and she talks
to the bears about staying away
from campgrounds, trash cans,
and foolishly daring people. . . .
She isn't brave, Tío explains,
just educated and wise.

I want to ask more about the way
he looks at her, but I'm too shy
to talk about feelings.

The next day, at school,
I'm exhausted. Since the kids
in my class are different ages,
I get to work at my own pace.
Slowing down really helps.
If only there was some way
to make my shadowy
fear of the future
slow down too.

Maybe I would feel brave
in this classroom of strangers
if I had a loud voice like Gracie
and could ask nosy questions,
but I don't. I'm quiet
and scared,
so finally, I dare myself
to try
something new.
I accept the teacher's offer

to help Gracie write online articles
about search-and-rescue dogs
like Gabe—their elaborate training,
their dedicated handlers,
all the human-canine
teamwork
and courage.

I've seen a few of Gracie's articles,
and I don't know how I'll ever manage
to write in that confident tone,
so I just decide to write the way I think,
with bursts of alternating
dread
and hope.

Online, I study Gracie's choice
of topics. There's a funny piece
about a local robbery. Peaches
were stolen from a cabin. The sheriff
found evidence: a smashed window,
an overturned table, and a trail
of peach juice smeared

on huge paw prints
that proved the burglar
was a bear.

The next article is sad. Old folks
at a retirement home told Gracie
that the one thing that's changed
the most since they were young
is fences. They can remember
crossing mountains in any direction,
limited only by rocky cliffs,
wild rivers,
and time.

Now, at night, my dreams
are filled with the spiky fences
around fighting-dog kennels

and the electrified ones
around prisons

and the wall between Mom's mind
and mine.

Will there ever be any way
to leap or climb over
that invisible height?

At school, language-arts hour
is a relief from worries
and dream-fears
and math.

The poetry assignment feels
easy and free. Maybe words
are my strength.
I could turn out to be
a superhero
with secret
syllable powers.

I want to keep my poem quiet,
but Gracie volunteers to read
her verse out loud. It's a funny
rhymed poem about visiting
her parents in India
and making huge, fruity Popsicles
for elephants—each one has a funny,

way of eating
a bucket-size ice ball.
Some stomp and gobble.
Others nibble delicately.
There's one—Gracie's favorite—
that lifts the ice and lets it melt
on top of his head, so he can reach
up, up, up
with his trunk
to pluck huge chunks
of mangos and melons
at leisure.

My quiet poem is about waiting.
I write it from Gabe's
energetic dog point of view,
imagining how he feels
when he's eager to work
and anxious to play
even though he's been
commanded to stay.

The teacher says it's good,
and when I ask her to please

never make me read it out loud,
she's nice enough to agree.

After that, school isn't too bad,
but by the time spring break
comes around, I'm ready for time off.
Gabe time. Dog time. Dirty, dusty,
rolling around in grass time.
Laughing, adventurous forest time.
Tío time. Family time.
Each time I think of my uncle
and his dog as a real family,
I have to correct myself.
Remind myself.
Foster family.
Temporary.
Fragile.

Spring break means riding
around in the truck
from one campground to another,
listening to Tío as he leads nature hikes
on trails so remote and beautiful

that I hardly even notice
the bear tracks.

We sleep in a tent, Gabe's snorts
and my uncle's snores blending
like a chorus of weird, funny music.

Life in a tent feels so different
that it's easy for me to pretend
I'm on an expedition
in a magical land
where nightmares don't exist
and all the dreams
are peaceful.

During Tío's nature hikes, I learn
how to recognize rattlesnakes,
poison oak, and wild foods.
If you're lost in the forest,
wilderness lore says you can eat miner's lettuce
and certain lily roots,
but not camas lilies.
You can make fishing line

from stinging-nettle fibers,
ink from pigeon berries,
chewing gum from sugar pine sap.

By the second day of spring break,
I know more about wilderness
than I ever knew about my own
scary home
in the city.

Mountain lion tracks
have a letter *m* at the base
of each paw print.
A snake moving fast
usually makes a zigzag print,
while a slow, relaxed snake
tends to leave a straight line.
A bear's short front feet
leave tracks that look a lot
like a big dog's paw prints,
but the long back feet of a bear
leave eerie shapes that almost
look human.

By the third day of spring break,
I've learned that yellow-bellied marmots
resemble giant squirrels, but they chew wires
under the hoods of cars, leaving campers
stranded and furious.

If a painted lady butterfly lands
on your nose, it's tasting your skin,
drinking salt.

When lightning is about to strike,
wilderness lore says your hair stands up, just like
in old cartoons, so you have to
plant your feet wide apart
and curl your body downward,
and tuck your head so you're not
tall and skinny like a lightning rod.

It's the opposite with mountain lions.
If you see one, reach up and stretch—
try to look big and brave.
Don't turn your back or run.
Never look like prey.

Each night, in the tent, I review
newly memorized wildflowers.
Fireweed, paintbrush, sky pilot.
Names designed
for dreaming.

By the time spring break ends,
I feel so close to Tío that I'm afraid
to return to the cabin and break
the wild spell.

But Easter morning at Cowboy Church
feels dreamlike too. The sunrise service
begins with a horseback drill-team dance.
Gracie is in the lead, galloping at full speed
around and around,
performing pirouettes
and figure eights.

I sit on the corral fence,
wondering how long it takes
to learn full-gallop courage.

Gabe is busy with other dogs,
but Tío and B.B. are nearby,
talking and smiling like they might
turn out to be a lot more
than friends.
The thought makes me cringe.
If Tío married B.B., would Gracie
be my stepniece?

Luckily, I have better things
to think about, because later that same day,
all of us pack a picnic and drive to a grove
of giant sequoia trees. I stand at the base
of one of the oldest, most enormous
living things in the world,
a tree so huge that one branch
looks as big
as a whole
peaceful
forest.

The calmness I absorb in that grove
stays with me for days, until Mom

suddenly starts calling to apologize
for avoiding my visit.

She claims it's the fault of lifers
who keep trying to lure her
into fights so she'll get in real trouble
and end up with a life sentence
like theirs.

I don't know why she bothers
to dump her prison troubles on me.
She can't be dumb enough to fall
into another fighting trap.
She'll probably get out on time,
and then she'll want me back,
and I'll have to go

but I can't imagine
giving up Gabe.

Maybe I could sneak him away
with me . . . .

but then he'd have to
learn how to fight
against pit bulls,
and that would
make me

even more greedy
and selfish

than Mom.

I'd be
a monster
a nightmare

impossible

no.

10 GABE THE DOG
TOGETHERNESS

I don't understand sadness,
but I can smell the way it makes
the boy feel unnaturally heavy,
so that his breath doesn't seem
to be made
of air.

It's an odor that rhymes
with the weight of aloneness,
so I press my head against the palm
of his hand, hoping to help him feel
the floating lightness
of never-lonely.

TONY THE BOY
THE RESCUE BEAST

Tío notices my mood.
He invites me to talk, but I don't feel
ready, so he takes me with him
out to the woods, where I help him
by hiding for his search-and-rescue team
of volunteer handlers and their dogs.

Hiding offers me a strange escape
from feeling cheated by life,
even though the dog handlers call me
a volunteer victim.

The way they say it, victim sounds so useful,
because it means that when I hide

in the forest, all the dogs have a chance
to practice finding a real victim.

There are all sorts of complicated
training exercises, but the simplest
is the first one every SAR dog learns:
a runaway.

All I have to do is race away
from a dog as it watches me.
The handler holds on to its collar
so it can't follow until I've vanished
behind a tree or a boulder.

Once I'm out of sight, the dog
is turned loose, and the handler
shouts, Find!

The eager dog rushes
to do his playful
hide-and-seek work,
running to my hiding place
so that he can receive

two rewards—his handler's praise
and a treat, or a toy.

Even the most experienced dogs
love to do runaways
just for fun,
but they also need
more difficult problems.
It's like they're doing math,
and they already know fractions,
percentages, and word problems,
so now they have to move on
and try to master
prealgebra.

Dogs don't separate reality
from fantasy. It's all the same,
all work, all play. Imagine a world
where homework is fun. That's
a dog's world. Just thinking about it
encourages me. Maybe there's hope
for a kid who hates numbers.

Research for an online article
about SAR dogs
calms me too.
It helps me feel safe to know
that search-and-rescue volunteers
practice all year, just in case
someone gets lost.
Even a stranger.
Especially a stranger.

Tío risks his life each time he goes out
in wild weather, at night, in rough terrain,
to search for a child or a thru-hiker.

My uncle claims
he's not brave.

He says there's a fierceness
that takes over his mind, giving him
endurance and strength. He insists
that anyone who has ever
searched for the lost
knows how it feels
to be transformed

into a Rescue Beast
thinking of others
instead of himself.

Rescue Beasts are the opposite
of werewolves. They're people
who turn into wilderness heroes
instead of villains.

There's so much to know.
Where do I start? Tío advises me
to study the dogs, not the Beast.
He shows me how there are two kinds
of searches, area and trailing.
Gabe is one of the few dogs trained
to do both. When he zigzagged
all over the apple grove, his nose
was up in the air, searching for any
human scent, any human at all.
That's called area work.

Trailing work is different.
It can only be done when there's
a PLS—a place last seen—a spot

where someone saw the lost person
right before she vanished.
A trailing dog sniffs any object
that carries the victim's scent—a pillow,
a jacket, a hat. Whenever there's a PLS,
Gabe searches on a long leash,
like a bloodhound in a manhunt movie,
nose to the ground, following only one
set of footprints as he sniffs to match
the smell of those tracks
to the scent of the pillow.

It's eerie, thinking how easily we
can get lost and how little of ourselves
we leave behind. Sunglasses. A backpack.
Winter gloves. After a week or two,
even the unique smell of a person
is gone. The place last seen is only
fragrant and useful for a few days,
or at most, a few weeks. . . .
Thinking of lost people
reminds me of Mom, but instead
of letting me focus on loss,
Tío goes into Rescue Beast mode,

showing me how to concentrate
on helping others. On SAR training days,
a bunch of us gather in the forest, and I
have my chance to help the dogs
by hiding.

First, I'm escorted to a hiding place
by Tío, who gives me a two-way radio
so I can call him for help
if I get scared.

He marks the spot on his GPS—
a Global Positioning System gadget
that uses beams from satellites
out in space—to show him exactly
where I am at all times, so that even
if the most experienced dogs
and their handlers
happen to have a bad day,
I'll be found.

So I'm safe, and the forest sounds
are soothing, and there are squirrels
and birds to keep me from feeling
completely alone

and I know that no matter how long
I have to wait to be found, Gabe
and the other dogs will take turns

and while they're searching,
they'll learn how to find
real victims.

Even though I enjoy all that oddly
comforting quiet time, alone
and relaxed in the wild,
wondrous woods,
I'm always relieved to hear
the eager pop-pop-pop
of a panting dog's breath
as it races toward me,
helping me feel
like such an important
part of the heroic
Rescue Beast
team.

12 GABE THE DOG
TEAMWORK

All I need are my energetic nostrils
so I can follow
the hiding boy's
scent trail.

As soon as I find Tony, I run back to alert my Leo,
who follows close behind me, paying his own special
human attention, with eyes and mind instead of a smart,
twitching nose.

At the end of our practice search, all three of us
know that we've done our best seeking
and hiding.

13 TONY THE BOY LOSER

I would hide in the wilderness
forever if it meant avoiding
prison visits.

Mom's arms
are crisscrossed
by new tattoos
of paw prints.

As long as I can remember,
she's always had a few
dark blue designs
on her skin

but now there's a mark
for each fighting pit bull
that ever won a battle

and a teardrop
for each dog
that lost
its life.

Does she actually care
about the dogs that lost fights?

She used to call them losers,
the same name she gave me

each time
I tried

to turn away
from the sight
of blood.

I hate visiting the prison,
but each time Tío assures me

that I don't have to go, I always
decide to give Mom
one more chance.

I don't have much to say
when she chatters
on and on
about all her new
prison friends.

I don't even want her to know
Gracie's name.
Or Gabe's.

I come away from those visits
feeling like such a loser.

If I turned into a tattoo
on Mom's face,
I'd be
a teardrop.

14 GABE THE DOG
BOY TRAINING

How do I train a boy? I try to show him
how to be joyful just walking and running

and chasing
roundness

but each time Tony goes back down
to the flatlands

he comes home smelling
like sorrow.

15 TONY THE BOY
LONELY SMELLS

Prison visits are getting harder,
but helping Tío and Gabe solve
their search-and-rescue mysteries
has given me a new way to face
the mysterious side of math.

Compared with trying to figure out
how Mom's weird mind works,
school is almost easy.

Numbers aren't always scary anymore.
They don't have to remind me
of mean men betting
bad money
at dogfights.

I understand some types of problems,
if I go slow and count trees or rocks
instead of fangs
and claws.

Gabe tries to cure my worries
with demands. He needs attention.
I throw a tennis ball so many times
that my shoulder gets sore.
Then he wants to swim, dive, plunge,
paddle, drip, and shake.

All Labs love water.
Gabe swims like a dolphin.
I don't.

I'm terrified of depths. No one ever
taught me how to laugh when I splash,
so I sit on a creek bank while Gabe
plays in the water, begging me
to join him, begging me to leave
my safe shore.

Heart dry.
Mind dusty.
Over and over, I promise Gabe
that someday, somehow, I'll learn
how to swim with him so we can be
happy
together.

Back in the cabin, when the phone rings,
I'm secretly glad that it's a call-out
for a search. I know I shouldn't be glad
that a stranger is lost, but I need a chance
to show my uncle
that I can be trusted
to stay at base camp.

This time, the subject of the search
is a sad old man
who drove uphill,
far away from his room
in a nursing home.

He parked at a wilderness trailhead
and started walking away from his life.

A couple of Italian thru-hikers saw him
when he got out of his car,
so the driver's-side seat
is the place last seen.

Gabe is on a long leash, working
as a trailing dog. He sniffs the dusty
upholstery, inhaling the old man's
hospital scent, a mixture
of skin, soap, and medicine,
along with invisible clues
that only a dog's nose can detect—
adrenaline from excitement or fear,
and probably all sorts
of mysterious chemicals
produced by loneliness
and confusion.

Gabe matches the smell on the seat
to the only footprints
on this rugged trail
that were made by soft
bedroom slippers

instead of steel-toed
hiking boots.

I've learned to wait.
Hiding in the woods has made me
patient. Visiting Mom has helped me
want to help others—the people who
are willing to be helped.

I know I can be useful to Tío
by obeying his command to stay
at base camp, which, as usual,
is a sheriff's van and a table where B.B.
is in charge of deciding which
dog teams, horse teams, ATVs,
and ground pounders
will search the areas
not covered by Gabe.

Gracie chatters, but I hardly listen,
because I'm trying so hard
to imagine what it must be like
for Tío

out there
in the forest
where the old man
is lost.

Where does he find
his Rescue Beast courage?
When I'm his age, will I know
how to search?

I wait for hours.
By the time Gabe finds the old man,
he's hungry, dehydrated, weak,
and grateful.

He thought he wanted to die
alone in the woods, but now he's glad
to be alive and surrounded
by people who care.

I'm happy for him, but I'm also
happy for myself. In a small, quiet,
satisfying way, by hiding out in the woods

during training, I helped teach SAR dogs
how to save lives.

I also proved that I'm trustworthy.
Tío ruffles my hair with his hand,
and I grin when I imagine
that if Gabe could praise me,
he would probably shout,
Good human!

Instead, he rewards me
with a ball-chasing game
and the warm, brown
roundness
of his wise, happy
dog eyes.

16 GABE THE DOG SNIFFING SCHOOL

I search for the sad-scented old man.

I find him.

I win!

Now Tony wants to learn all my search games, so I
show him how my Leo teaches agility—

crawl through tunnels

climb up ladders

leap onto a seesaw

      while

           it

                moves

balance on a long, narrow beam   don't fall but

if you do tumble   don't be afraid   to try again

and   again   and   again.

I can teach obedience, too:

Come! Sit! Stay! Down! Heel (always on the left).

I also share what I know about NO.

NO chasing squirrels.

NO chasing rabbits.

NO chasing deer.

NO chewing boots.

Finally, I teach Tony to see how I get along

with other dogs, and I'm not afraid to jump

right into a roaring, whirling HELO, the helicopter

that takes me to other mountains

for faraway search games . . .

and when I'm through teaching

all that I know

about work-play

it's time to show the boy

how we can both

lie down and curl up

and rest.

17 TONY THE BOY
INSECT MATH

There are so many ways
to get lost. Each search is a surprise.
One day, an experienced outdoorsman
goes hiking alone, and when he doesn't
come home, his wife calls 911,
and the sheriff calls Tío.
By the time Gabe finds him,
he's feverish, his legs broken
and infected from a fall.

The next week, a teenage girl
separates from her friends,
promising to meet them
at the far edge
of a rocky slope.

She's hiking with flip-flops
instead of boots.
A tank top and shorts.
No jacket, no warmth.
She suffers hours of terror
all night, and then a swift burst
of relief.
when Gabe finally appears,
collar bell rattling,
orange vest glowing. . . .

Tío runs close behind Gabe,
offering the cold girl
a space blanket,
silvery and magical
like moonlight.

Panic. It's the topic of my next
online article. A lost person often
runs in circles, following the same
frantic pattern
over and over,
like an orbit around a planet
of hope.

Both Gracie and our teacher
love the article. They tell me
I've learned so much!

It's true. Gabe has helped me discover
new things each day. Dog truths.
People truths, too.
For instance,
there's this one
really great
prison visit,
the biggest surprise
of my new life,
because I never expected
to be able to smile
on the other side
of that heavy gate.

Mom looks cheerful,
and she acts
gentle.

Her hair is supershort.
She tells me she volunteered

to cut it and donate it to Wigs
for Kids with Cancer.

She's also started volunteering
to read books out loud
in a quiet room

with an easy chair
beside a red rose

in a blue vase.

She says that little room
is the only peaceful place
in the entire prison.

She describes the way her calm,
soothing voice
is recorded to make
listening books
for blind children.

She tells me that generous
volunteer projects
will help her get early parole,

and a new career helping people
instead of hurting dogs.

At first, I just feel amazed,
then hopeful, and finally,
so excited that I'm able to relax
and share a happy picnic with Mom
on the same sunny lawn
where women with incense
are singing.

That one good visit
feels like a joyful dream
until the next time, when
she doesn't even
show up and the social worker
warns me that Mom is fighting again,
insulting other prisoners,
hitting, hurting,
and getting
hurt.

I'm ferociously disappointed,
but I struggle fiercely
to concentrate on *now* instead of

the future. I try to pay attention.
Even in math. Tío helps me
with the numbers. It's the first time
anyone has ever looked
at my homework.

When you put Tío and math
together, you end up
way out in the wild forest.
I learn how to estimate
the temperature of soil
at a 6-inch depth
by counting beats
per minute
in the song
of a cricket.
Fast insect music
means the earth is warm.
Slow bug songs come only
on long, cold cricket nights.

Tío also shows me how to count
the age of a giant sequoia tree's
charred stump. Rings of growth

from ancient times. Wide rings
for spring, narrow ones
for summer
or drought years.

We punch mapping coordinates
into a GPS gadget, but it only works
if you're out in the open, with a clear path
to a satellite orbiting in space. The GPS
won't work if you hold it in a dark,
shadowy forest
where modern science
can't find you.

All the outdoor math lessons
are helping, and I'm really hoping
to get good grades. The semester's
almost over, and I can hardly wait
for summer, even though
it's going to be weird.
I'll have to spend weekdays
with B.B. while Tío is away at work
in distant campgrounds.

Luckily, loud Gracie won't be around
to make me feel
small.

She'll be far away, in India, visiting
her parents and the elephants.
I imagine she'll spend half her time
making elephant Popsicles
and the rest just trying to figure out
ways to come back bragging
about traveling so much farther
than prison.

B.B. is excited. She tells me
she's planning activities for me.
Sports, crafts, swimming lessons,
and bear whispering. . . .

Bear whispering? Bear whispering!
If only summer wasn't still two whole
seven-day weeks away! Math tests
are making me 50 percent crazy.

No cricket music or tree rings,
just the speed of airplanes

and other really hard word problems
that send 99 percent of my mind
flying away

flying into daydreams
about reaching
summertime

and the end
of tests.

My final-exam grade is a C.
Average! For the first time
in my entire life,
I haven't
completely
confusingly
failed.

The teacher smiles and tells me
she'll give extra credit
for a cricket-song essay
or a poem
about tree rings.

Tío must have talked to her.
He probably told her about the fights
and the bets
and the sad way I was always
the one who had to count dollars
and report the numbers
to Mom.

Dogs that didn't bring
a profit

lost a lot more
than money.

18 GABE THE DOG
DOG TRUTHS

At night, Tony lies awake,
stroking my head
and whispering
our
summer plans.

All I care about is the *our* word.
As long as we're together
time will feel round
and safe.

19 TONY THE BOY
UNO

Mountain chores are easy.
No decisions. No numbers.
No grown-up
responsibilities.
All I have to do is help my uncle
plant his garden,
pick fruit and vegetables,
chop firewood,
and cook berries
so that we can surprise
hungry thru-hikers
with fresh-baked pies,
a gift that leaves us chuckling,
because each adventurer

from Sweden, Canada, or Chile
can devour a whole pie
and still look hungry.

Cowboys on horseback
aren't starving, but they are
full of gratitude each time we drop off
a pie while they're herding cattle
up to high, peaceful meadows
that look like smooth green lakes.

Old cowboys help Tío teach me
wilderness lore. I learn that beaver houses
are built of sticks,
while muskrat lodges
are mostly mud.
I learn that fence lizards have smooth
blue bellies but newts on this mountain are warty red,
and I memorize natural patterns,
like the upside-down V
in the paw print
of a red fox—scientific name:
Vulpes vulpes.

I love it when life makes some sort
of orderly, organized sense, so:
I
        learn
                that
                        rabbits
                                bite
                                        twigs
at a clean forty-five-degree angle

while deer leave
shaggy
frayed tips

and porcupines shred the bark

but bears reach way up high
to rip claw marks
in tree trunks
maybe to show off
their
height
so that other bears
will respect them.

Summer arrives. I've passed math
and I know a lot about wilderness
and I feel
almost
as tall
and tough
as a bear,
but I don't have to be strong
around B.B., who lets me act young,
silly, funny, clumsy, and small
during my swimming lessons
with Gabe in a quiet pond
beneath a waterfall—
so cool
on hot days!

B.B.'s idea of a summer sport
is romping across a green meadow
with Gabe, and the crafts she shows me
are just animal and bird statues
that we make from all sorts of stuff
we find—pinecones, acorns, pebbles,
fossils, arrowheads, and feathers.

When I admit that I miss
writing online articles, B.B. helps me
start a blog, using a goofy, grinning photo
of Gabe as my canine coauthor.
At first, I want to call the blog
something complicated and scientific,
but then I decide that a simple name
like Dog Nose Notes
will make readers curious.

So I start writing SAR dog thoughts
as I imagine Gabe would write them
if he could: When you get lost
in the wondrous woods,
stay in one place. Don't wander.
Keep your scent trail simple,
because each roaming step you take
makes it harder for a dog's nose
to find you.

I even write about the sad part
of searching. Hardly any modern people
know how to stay alive in the wild

for more than a few desperate days.
If a lost hiker isn't found quickly,
Gabe has to use his cadaver dog training.
Finding bodies instead of survivors.
Tío calls it the monstrous side
of the Rescue Beast. Searchers
have to keep searching
even when they know
that too much time
has passed.

If I ever get lost, I'll want to survive,
so I beg Tío to let me tag along
when he teaches apprentice handlers
how to prepare for their big, scary
UNO.

In Spanish, *uno* just means one,
but in the daring language
of search-and-rescue volunteers,
it means "unexpected night out."
SAR dog handlers learn to survive
without a sleeping bag or a fire.
No easy warmth. No cooked meals.

Just a little imagination
and a lot of courage.

So I pretend I'm a real searcher,
trapped by wild weather.
I make a shelter of leafy branches,
and I reinvent the sleeping bag
by stuffing pine needles into a trash bag.
I eat miner's lettuce, berries,
and cattail shoots sweetened
with sugar-pine sap.

It's eerie spending a cold night
outdoors, close to Gabe but so far
from people. Well, not too far—Tío
is camped really close by,
and even though it's hard to find
a cell phone signal out here,
he has a satellite phone
for emergencies,
and we have two-way radios
so he can call to ask if I'm okay,
and I can answer, first saying copy,
to let him know that I hear him,

then, over when I'm through,
promising that I'm fine.
I feel like I'm in an adventure movie,
talking like a bush pilot
or an explorer!

While Gabe and I are out
in the darkness, I start to wonder
if he wants to leave and run back
to Tío, but he's a generous dog.
He takes care of me.
He stays close, snuggling
to keep both of us safe
and warm.

It's easy to sense
how divided

a dog
feels

when he loves
two people

and longs to be loyal
to both

but he knows
he has to choose

only one.

20 GABE THE DOG
SMELLY RHYMES

The scent of a whole night with Tony, far away from
   my Leo,
almost rhymes with an aroma of fear, but it's also
   a fragrance
of excitement, so I stay awake

until I sleep

and then I dream
the scent
of running

a wild smell that rhymes
with home.

21 TONY THE BOY
WALKING WITH BEARS

On summer mornings
out in the fragrant woods,
I learn to identify
the musky stench
of a black-bear den
in a hollow tree

but the wildest drifts
of clear mountain air

carry sounds
not just scent

an eerie cry, a screech, a moan—
soaring eagle

or slinking ghost?
It could be the protective cry
of a mountain lion mother
calling to her cubs. . . .

or La Gritona, La Llorona,
screaming woman, weeping woman,
a spirit from Tío's campfire tales
about a mother who shrieks
because her children are lost.

Mountain lions and spooky myths
are noisy, but studying bears
is mostly a matter
of silence.

When B.B. takes me out to help
with her research, poor Gabe
can't go with us, because even
the biggest bears love peace
and quiet. They run away
from barking dogs.

On my first day of wildlife biology,
we find ourselves face-to-face

with an adult male black bear
whose shaggy brown hair
makes me wonder why he's called
a black bear. B.B. explains
that they can be reddish
or light or dark. They can be
the same brown as grizzlies,
only smaller and a lot less
aggressive.

The bear points his long nose
and gives a soft woof, a warning
that sounds like a funny cross
between a sneeze and a bark.

We follow at a distance as he shuffles
from tree to tree, scratching roots
and gobbling
squirmy ant larvae.

B.B. speaks to the bear calmly,
advising him not to worry yet,
because hunting season won't start
until September.

Hunting? I can't believe that any
modern person would kill a bear.
Why? Are they hungry enough to need
bear meat, or is it a so-called sport
like a dogfight? Why do some people
keep trying to prove their strength?
If Mom was a hunter,
would she kill the world's
last bear?

Remembering my life before forests—
before wildlife and a gentle dog,
and gentle people—
I start to feel
so lonely

that I have to shove memories
of my old life
away

replacing them with B.B.'s scientific
attention to detail as she shows me
the colors of bear scat—that's a biologist's
way of saying *poop*. Blue scat means a bear

Elderberries

Blackberries

Manzanita

might have munched elderberries. Purple
could be from wild blackberries, and red
might be manzanita.

That evening, I post a Dog Nose blog entry
about bear behavior, along with a list
of wild foods. Blue and purple berries
are often safe, but white and yellow
are usually risky. There aren't any rules
for red. Wild strawberries are fine,
but some red berries are deadly.
Some things in life just can't be
predicted.

The subject of safety catches my interest,

so I do some research, then post a list
of foods that can poison dogs:
grapes, raisins, onions, garlic,
macadamia nuts, chocolate.
Gabe is called a chocolate Lab
only because his rich brown color
is warm and happy, not because
it would be fine if you gave him

a candy bar. He'd get convulsions.
He could die. Writing about danger
makes me worry—what would I do
if anything ever
happened to Gabe?

He sniffs my hand, as if he can smell
the invisible fingerprint
of my thoughts.

I wish we could both smell
the future.

22 GABE THE DOG
CHASING THE MOON

Tony talks about a future,
but I don't know what he means,
so we go outdoors, where he throws
a yellow glow-in-the-dark ball.

When a foolish squirrel runs
right in front of me, I don't chase it
very far, because my teeth are already
biting
the brightness
of my light-catching
moon wish.

I can't imagine ever needing
to do anything but play, right here,
right now, together.

23 TONY THE BOY
DANCING ELEPHANTS

Gracie sends a note of approval
all the way from India, shouting
an all-caps BRAVO! for my bear-
and-berry entry in the Dog Nose blog.

She adds an animal note of her own,
a poem called "Elephant Step Dance,"
about the way the soles of huge feet
can hear the drummed vibrations
of elephant messages
made by stomping
boom boom
on dry
hard
earth.

The poem is funny, but is it true?
I rush to find out, and my research
tells me that yes, elephant feet
really do act like extra ears,
absorbing sounds.

I picture loud Gracie
on the other side of the world,
making sure that her own
booming voice
is heard
in verse.

A few days later, there's another
useless phone call from Mom.
Gracie's poetic drum rhythm
helps me think about my own
pounding fury
each time I have to hear
the lies.

The last time I went to the prison,
I was
the silent

sullen
one

but now
I'm noisy
and vicious.

Anger is like a disease.
You can catch it.
You can give it.

24 GABE THE DOG
THE SMELL OF A VOICE

When Tony yells into the phone,
I run and hide
in a dark
closet—
my cave. . . .

I won't come out. I won't.
Yelling isn't like thunder, far away in high sky.
Screaming is close. A shouting voice hurts.
I feel the slap of each word
as it spills
the bitter odor
of danger
into my nose.

25 TONY THE BOY
FOUND AND LOST

Loser, loser, loser! I feel so terrible
about scaring Gabe by yelling at Mom
over the phone. I feel so horrible,
so awful, so lost!

But Gabe forgives me right away.
He always forgives everyone.
If Tío gets mad at him for breaking
the No Chasing Squirrels rule,
they make up quickly, but I never
seem to get over things
swiftly
and easily
like a trusting dog

or a really smart
grown-up.

Why does 50 percent of my mind
always seem to be stuck
in unhappy mode?

There's only one way
to take my thoughts away from
Mom's prison cell of rage.
Searches. Finding the lost. Helping.

My uncle tells me that before
the invention of GPS gadgets,
there were searches almost every day.
Hardly anyone knew what to do
with a compass and map, or how
to navigate by the stars.

Now, with GPS and fancy new
satellite phones that can get a signal
anywhere—even in the most remote
wild places—lost hikers often call

forest rangers
to ask which trail to choose
at a crossroads.

With all the modern technology,
wilderness searches are needed
only once in awhile, but they're
still just as urgent as before.
Life or death. All or nothing.

One night, an autistic teenager
wanders away from a cabin.

The next week, two fishermen
fail to find the trail back downhill
from a high mountain lake.

A Swiss thru-hiker is rescued
when he gets disoriented
from dehydration.

There are crime scenes, too,
searches so gross that Tío won't
let me hang out at base camp.

All I know is what I hear later,
when he and B.B. talk,
holding hands.

As soon as I see
how their fingers
touch

I start to wonder
what will happen to me
if they
get married.

My uncle's cabin is too small
for all of us.

How long will it be
until he sends me away?

Every time I start believing
in safety,
something happens

that makes me feel
like an old toothbrush
in the lost-
and-found
box
at school.

Nobody wants someone else's
trash.

26

GABE THE DOG
SHARING

Tony smells
so lonely
that I try
to share
my food
my water
my toys

but all he wants is company
so I take him outside and we run
round and round in dizzy circles
until finally, we fall down
and laugh
together.

27 TONY THE BOY
SHORELINES

Summer turns into a season
of mysterious migrations.

One morning, there are thousands
of bright red ladybugs.
The next day, it's shiny blue dragonflies,
swooping across soft green meadows.
Suddenly, only the tiniest spiders
float overhead, each one dangling
from a natural parachute
of silky white web.

Roaming wild creatures
don't worry about where
they'll end up, but I do,

I really do worry, so when Tío
invites me on a vacation road trip
to a distant beach, I'm excited,
but I'm also not sure how I feel
about leaving the comforting
mountains.

We ride with open windows,
Gabe and I both sniffing the breeze
as we zoom right past the prison,
turning west, then driving, gliding,
until we finally reach the bright,
endless ocean, and the warm,
sun-gold sand.

When Gabe chases shore birds
into frothy waves, I follow, running
and splashing, even though I know
I'll never be able to catch any creature
with wings.

I don't even want to catch birds,
but it feels so great to act like a tiny
kid again, romping with new puppies

that have never
been hurt.

Pelicans slide across the bright sky.
Sea otters roll around on blue water.
Everything is so peaceful
that I wonder if it's possible
to feel sad and scared
on any beach
anywhere
in the huge world.

That night, under brilliant stars,
I ask my uncle a question
that I've wondered about
for a long time.

How did he feel when he floated away
from his home island? What was it like,
drifting on a raft in a storm,
then wrecking, being washed ashore
in a nameless place, without food
or a dog. . . .

I can't picture my uncle before Gabe.
They belong together—how did Tío survive?

After a long, quiet moment, he speaks
of his childhood on the troubled island
where he had to be careful about rules.
Strange rules. Censored books.
Rationed food. Secret police.
Neighborhood spies.
By the time he was a teenager,
he was in trouble with the authorities
for buying bread on the black market
and for reading forbidden stories
and listening to outlawed radio stations
that played illegal foreign music.

Illegal music? No wonder my uncle
and Mom both fled their homeland.
Did she listen to the wrong songs too?
Was she always a rule breaker?
Was there a time when she knew
which rules deserved breaking?

Tío goes on to describe his parents—
my grandparents. They aren't alive

anymore, but when I ask, my uncle says
maybe someday he'll be able to take me
back to the island, to meet all my cousins.

The story of Tío's youth ends
with his escape from the secret police,
on a homemade raft, in hurricane season.
Then the sea, the wreck, being stranded
on that nameless spit of sand, and finally,
surviving on rainwater, shellfish,
and seaweed. After a fisherman
found him, rescue became Tío's passion.
Nature had fed him, God and people
helped him. He was determined to do
the same for someone else.
He received asylum in Florida,
learned English, studied forestry,
then worked in the Everglades,
Yellowstone, and Yosemite,
before choosing to patrol
the most remote places
along the Pacific Crest Trail,
places that seemed almost
as vast and perilous
as an ocean.

Wherever he went, he always
experimented with wild foods
and survival skills. He experimented
with wild feelings, too, trying out
different emotions
the way people in cities
try on clothes.

He had to decide which feelings
could be trusted
and which ones would poison
his mind.

Anger was useless, fear deadly,
and despair was the most dangerous
emotion of all. He realized that hope
was the only feeling strong enough
to keep him alive.

When Tío falls silent, I gaze up
at beach stars, gather my courage,
and ask about Mom.

What was she like when she was little?
Did she fight, was she cruel, did she care
about people and puppies?

My uncle's answer makes me feel
as clear and limitless
as the starry sky.

Mom was ordinary.
Something changed her.
But she could change back.
And I'm not like her.
I'll always be free
to be myself.

28 GABE THE DOG
BEACH DREAMS

Sleeping in a tent on the moon-bright sand
I dream
swim-run-swim

and in the morning
I can still smell the dreams
of my Leo and Tony

because they were swimming with me
so that even alone on the water
I was never
alone.

29 TONY THE BOY
WHEN ELEPHANTS JUMP

By the time we drive back
from our cool beach vacation,
I've collected a few experimental
feelings of my own

along with sand dollars
and seashells

and a gooey bag of chewy
saltwater taffy for Gracie,
who's due back from India.

She arrives in a loud burst
of hilarious jungle poem-stories
about elephant sunscreen (mud)

elephant pizza (squashed trees)
and elephant dreams (jumping,
because when they're awake,
elephants are the only mammals
that can't leap).

After her welcome-home
nonelephant pizza party,
all I expect to do is sleep,
but a call-out comes at midnight,
and Tío takes me with him.
I wait restlessly at base camp,
wondering if I'll ever master
the frustrating art
of patience.

The lost person is a teenage boy
with a homemade bow and arrow.
There is no place last seen—so Gabe
has to search a huge area, off leash
and eager, as he races against time,
because the boy is diabetic, and if he
doesn't get his medicine,
he'll die.

His family brings candles, food,
flowers, and a makeshift altar.
They pray in a language I can't identify.
The women wear colorful dresses,
and somehow, the worried men
manage to look strong
and helpless
at the same time.

The search goes on and on,
but this time, Gabe isn't the hero.
A helicopter pilot makes the find,
spotting the lost boy from midair.
Exhausted but happy, Tío assures me
that search and rescue is teamwork,
not individual
glory.

Still, as I think about how hard
Gabe tried, I can't help but wonder
if SAR dogs ever feel
discouraged.

Lately, my mind is so full
of questions
that there doesn't seem to be room
for answers.

Wondering and wishing are all
I can manage at Cowboy Church,
where I try and try to pray
for Mom . . .

but end up feeling
like wondering and wishing
are better than seeing her

or opening her hopelessly
angry letters.

Now I know
how elephants must feel
in between their lively
jumping dreams

while they're awake
and limited
to plodding.

30 GABE THE DOG
MY WISHFUL NOSE

I'm not discouraged, just tired
and restful.

My nose has wishful moods
when the nostrils imagine sniffing
adventurous smells that I can't quite name
with my dog-words.

Tony, you look wishful too.
Does your boy nose dream
of exploring wild scent trails
in unknown air?

31 TONY THE BOY
DOG YEARS

Summer is the best cure
for worries. I'm so tired and relaxed
from swimming, hiking, playing
dog games, and learning bear facts
that I can almost sleep
straight through one whole
nightmare-free night.

Maybe that's why my dog nose blog
grows more confident
and number-rich
each day,
as I learn that people shed 40,000
skin cells per hour, creating a trail
of scent that a long dog nose

can follow, using all 230 million
scent receptors—100,000 times more
sniffing ability than the amount
of smell-skill in a short human nose.

It sounds like magic,
but it's science.

If I want to study wildlife biology,
or forestry, or veterinary medicine,
I'll need plenty of courage
to explore the tangled
wilderness of math.

So I try to copy Gabe's way of facing
each day with the energy of a dog's
excitement about work-play.
When I hide for SAR dog practice,
I notice the way all dogs love
adventure, but they also need to know
what to expect. Border collies
try to herd me, German shepherds
guard me, and Labs like Gabe
just love to fetch me.

I'm still trying to figure out how
playful dogs turn into such fiercely
loyal Rescue Beasts
while having so much fun.
Is there a mathematical formula
to explain generosity?

Tío and the other volunteer
SAR dog handlers are just as amazing.
They have normal jobs in forests, shops,
and offices, but as soon as they reach
a place last seen, they start to seem
like people from a different century—
a time when anyone could get lost
in the wild, and everyone always
joined the search posse.

I want to be just like them.
I crave that brave combination
of beastly toughness
and rugged kindness.

It's like moss on a boulder,
hard and soft at the same time,

the same blend I'll need if I'm ever
going to be a smart animal doctor
who knows how to cure
wounded dogs.

With thoughts of college and vet school,
I start seeing regular school
as important.
The new semester is a challenge
I almost feel ready to face.
Same classroom, same teacher,
same friendly students,
but I hardly recognize the girls.
They look a lot older, and they act
all giggly—even Gracie, who has grown
supertall, weirdly shy, and surprisingly
pretty.

But girls aren't my only confusion.
On September 15, the first day
of Hispanic Heritage Month,
the teacher asks me to speak
to the whole class about my family
and their origins.

But I wasn't born on the island.
I'm American.
I barely know any Spanish.
How can I tell quaint, folksy tales
about fiestas, feasts, cousins,
and grandmas. . . .

I won't do it.
I don't belong.
Not here.
Or anywhere.
I can't belong.
Ever.

When I refuse to speak,
the teacher says she understands,
but then Gracie jumps in
and invites Tío to talk in my place.
He agrees, but only after asking me
if it's okay. I do mind. I mind a lot,
but I don't want to hurt his feelings,
so I keep my anxiety
secret.

I find myself listening with laser-sharp ears
as Tío tells the whole class about his life.
My eyes feel blurry, and my mind
has left the room. All I can think about
is Mom hungry, Mom scared,
Mom on a raft, drifting. . . .

Why didn't I ever ask about
her childhood?

If I ask now, will she answer
and if she does, will her answers
be honest?

My birthday is coming soon—maybe
that will be the perfect chance to try
to get to know more
about Mom's weird past . . .
but on the day when I finally
turn twelve, there's no card or call,
no proof that I ever had a mother.

No prison visit either,
but that's my choice.

Tío bakes a carrot cake, and gives me
a brand-new laptop, and the warmest
hug
of my life.

Then B.B. gives me a grinning
photo of Gabe, a picture that brings tears
of happiness to my eyes, but I don't
actually cry, because Gracie chooses
that moment to give me a silly poem

about the clumsy way
baby elephants play
while they're learning
how to control all 40,000
clunky muscles
in their trunkies.

After that, we sing and howl off-key.
It's the first time anyone has ever
called my birthday
happy.

This story of turning twelve will be great,
when I tell it on my dog nose blog,
with my new laptop, using plenty
of numbers that no longer remind me
of winners and losers
in long-ago fights.

When I sit down to write,
I say that Gabe is exactly half my age,
but he's also 6 times 7 = 42,
old and wise
in dog years—almost ancient—

but age doesn't stop him
from celebrating. All through
my whole birthday, he's the one
who helps me laugh
by grinning
as we gobble
messy frosting.

If only birthdays could last
forever. But they don't last.
Nothing lasts. Suddenly,
the forest
is no longer
peaceful.

32 GABE THE DOG
EXPLOSIONS

Each boom rhymes
with the smell
of danger.
Worse than thunder.
Worse than yelling.
I would hide in the closet
forever
if my Leo didn't keep patting me
and reminding me
that it's just the same
mean noise
we hear
every year.

33

TONY THE BOY
TRAIL NAMES

Hunting season opens
with gunfire at dawn.

Frightened deer hide
in our vegetable garden.

A desperate bear scratches
at the cabin door.

At first Gabe hides, but then
he goes crazy with fear, barking
and growling. He sounds like
a pit bull. He sounds
like Mom.

Gunshots and snarls
bring old nightmares
rushing back.
Why do I always
have to start over
again
and again
struggling
to be free
of the past?

Tío shakes me awake to say
that he's leaving, and at first
I assume he means forever . . .
but it's just another call-out
for a search.

As usual, I go with my uncle
to a safe base camp at a trailhead,
even though this time, the forest
is scary.

Hunting season means danger
for searchers, who have to keep

their dogs close, and make noise
with whistles, to warn hunters
who might otherwise mistake
any movement
for a deer
or a bear.

When I find out that Tío and Gabe
have to search for a lost hunter
who went out with six hounds,
I'm furious. Hunting doesn't
seem fair, to either the dogs
or the bear.

Bear hounds are trained to follow
a scent, running so fast and so far
that they often get lost. Even dogs
get mixed up when a chase is swift
and frenzied. Dog noses are smart,
but not perfect.

Bear hounds are supposed to chase
a bear up a tree, where it's easy
to shoot. This time, one of the hounds

got lost, and then the frantic hunter
lost his way too, running around,
trying to find his missing dog.

Now, the hunter's wife
is at base camp, crying
and complaining
about his dangerous
way of enjoying
the outdoors.

I look around at B.B., Gracie,
the sheriffs, and volunteers.
Everyone looks busy and useful
except me.

All I can think about is the hound.
I feel a lot more troubled by the thought
of a helpless dog than by the image

of a lost hunter
who still has his gun.

Instead of waiting by the crowded
base camp table, I start wandering

with a flashlight, hoping to see
canine paw prints.

Still hoping, I roam farther
and farther, first on the main trail,
then narrower paths that fade
until suddenly, I know
I've messed up.

Now I'm lost too.
There's no trail at all.
I'm surrounded by wildness.

That's how it happens—
one path leads to another.
So you choose, you walk,
you choose again,

and pretty soon,
there's no
turning back.

I don't have a GPS, or even a map
and compass. I hardly know anything
about navigation by starlight.

I don't have a two-way radio
or my cell phone, which probably
wouldn't even get a signal
way out here.

So I can't call for help.
I'm stuck waiting. I know the rules.
A lost person should stay in one place,
hug a tree, avoid wandering
in wider and wider
aimless
circles. . . .

Instead, I panic and run
until I'm sliding down
a long, steep
s
  l
    o
      p
       e
scrambling
to keep from falling
over a cliff.

This is stupid.
I should know better.
I might not always listen
to every boring grown-up rule,
but I am old enough to have
common sense.

So I make myself stop.
I stand motionless,
waiting.

The forest is crowded with SAR dogs
and searchers. If B.B. and the other
ground pounders don't find me,
then Gabe and Tío surely will.
Won't they?

I sit with my back against
an incense cedar tree,
where the red bark smells
like the smoky air
around those praying women
in the prison yard—thick air

clouded with incense
and gloom.

So many emotions churn
through my head that I feel
like a baby elephant
trying to learn how to use
its long
clumsy nose.

On my birthday, I never
would have guessed that twelve
could feel so young
and small
and complicated.

Anger. At myself. At Mom.
Terror. Of being lost forever.
Or getting found, and then
punished. Sent far away
to live with strangers.
Shame too.
How could I be so selfish?
Searchers who should be focused
on finding the hunter and his hound
will have to waste time
looking for me.

Or will they? Has anyone
even noticed
that I'm gone?

Sitting still with these thoughts
becomes impossible, so I lurch
to my feet, and stumble back

the way I came. Or at least I hope
it's the way. Panic makes the world
shaky. Things seen from a distance
change shape as I move closer—
a loping coyote turns out to be
a motionless slab of granite.
That soaring pterodactyl
is just a crow.
Tall
skinny
ancient
people
wearing
flowing
robes
are
only
brown
tree
trunks.

I race, then trudge, knowing I can't
even trust my own eyesight . . .
but at least the night is over.
Daytime strikes like lightning.

I've been lost for hours and hours. . . .
I run, walk, run again
until I'm so exhausted
that all I can do
is stop and rest,
wish, hope, pray,
and think of Gabe's
smart nose
warm fur
happy grin
loyalty
courage.

But the weather is turning.
Blue sky goes cloudy.
A cold wind shrieks
like the spirits
in one of Tío's spooky
campfire stories.

I close my eyes, hoping that when
I open them, I'll discover that I've been
dreaming.

Is that musky scent
a bear's?

Am I touching
fur?

When I open my eyes, instead of dreams,
I discover a reddish dog who whines
as he greets me, nuzzles my arm,
and shows me his trusting eyes,
filled with joy and hope, because now
that he's found a human, he assumes
everything will be fine.

It's not Gabe or another SAR dog,
so it must be the hunter's hound.
He's lean and bony.
How long has he been out here?
Two days? Three? I've lost
track of time. I'm hungry,
so the poor dog must be
starving.

I can't believe that while I was
searching for him, he's the one
who ended up finding me.

I feel like a cave boy.
This is how it must have been.
Tío has told me about coevolution,
like when hummingbird beaks
gradually changed shape, just to fit
certain flowers. Dogs and man
learned to need each other
thousands of years ago.
No wonder I suddenly feel
like I'm home,
even though I'm still
out in the woods,
lost and cold.
Scared.

The hound is weak, but he talks
to me in his dog-language
of movement and touch.
B.B. has told me that wild animals

don't make eye contact, because
they don't need to understand
human faces, but dogs do need
to know us. They can't live
alone.

This hound is so friendly,
and he must have a name.
I try out a few, but he wiggles
happily, no matter what I say.
Angel, Magic, Wizard.
I make my voice high
and squeaky
so it sounds excited.

My approval is the dog's
reward.

Suddenly, I feel hopeful. Ever since
I learned about trail names,
I've wondered what I'd call myself
if I'm ever brave enough
to be a thru-hiker.

Rescue Beast. No—Trail Beast!
That's what I'd be, part Trail Angel
and part mysterious,
ferociously dedicated,
educated, scientific,
magical. . . .

34 GABE THE DOG
SEARCH!

I'm tired, but we have a place where Tony was last
seen, and we have a scent object—his backpack—so I
plunge my nose in, sniffing his boy-life of games, paper,
ink, and sweet treat snacks. . . .

Then I tug the long leash to keep my Leo close behind
me as I inhale shoe prints, nose to the ground,
following tracks, so I can

find

find

find

our Tony.

Nothing else matters.

35 TONY THE BOY RESCUED!

The hound is too weak
to walk, and too heavy to carry,
so I stay still, hugging him,
even though I desperately
want to run and search for berries and a stream.

Hunger.
Thirst.
Fear.

Now I know how Tío felt
when his raft
was drifting.

How long can a dog live
without any food and water?

If it gets colder, my fingers
and toes will be numb.

If only Tío or B.B. would find us.
They both know all sorts
of human and canine first aid.

Sounds in the forest grow
eerily loud
when you're lost.
The wing beat of a raven
is like thunder
or a monstrous roar

so when I hear a collar bell
that tinkles like Christmas
and I see the orange flash
of a SAR dog's happy vest,

and I feel the familiar warmth
of Gabe's panting breath,

I feel so relieved
and so safe

that I finally crumple up
and cry.

Gabe licks me, Tío hugs me,
and the hunter's hound rolls over
to show Gabe that he's
not a fighter. The two dogs
sniff each other curiously.
It's some sort of diplomacy,
like when the presidents of countries
shake hands on TV.

If I'm going to be a veterinarian,
I'll have to learn as much as I can
about the sign language dogs use
to talk to each other—this joyful
dance of wagging tails,
lolling tongues, thrashing legs,
and wiggly bellies.

After that, my mind is a blur.
Base camp, then the truck, a clinic,
good news: the bear hound
will survive, and the hunter

was found by one of the dogs
that has practiced finding me
over and over, when I was just
a volunteer victim
pretending
to be lost.

The rest of that first day at home
is so peaceful and cozy
that I can't imagine
ever going outdoors again.

All I want is soup
cookies
hot cocoa
and sleep.

The next day, I feel strong enough
to accept Tío's after-breakfast lecture
without any arguments. He's right.
I should have stayed at base camp.
I should have listened
and cooperated.

We spend the rest of the morning
relaxing, and then, after lunch,
we go online together, and we order
a fancy new satellite phone
so that I'll never again be stranded
in any rugged, remote area
where old-style cell phones
can't get a signal.

But the biggest gift
my uncle gives me
is the calm, patient feeling
that I still have plenty of time
to learn
common sense.

It's just like math, he promises.
Just learn one formula at a time.
The first is such a simple rule
that you'll never forget:
DON'T HIKE ALONE.

My lost-and-found mood
of grateful relief
lasts until Halloween.

That's when everything
suddenly
turns mean and scary.

One final prison visit.
Mom is a no-show.

The nightmares come back
with such hurricane force
that I know I'm facing
a decision.

This is my life.
My chance.
My only hope.

I'm at a crossroads, a place
where two paths meet.
There aren't any road signs
telling me which trail
will lead toward a future
and which could carry me back
into my past.

I can choose to continue
feeling like one of Mom's
doomed puppies

or I can let my mind
take that first step
toward safety.

So I tell the social worker
to stop scheduling me for prison visits.,
and I tell Tío that I'm tired of waiting
for Mom
to grow up.
I'm ready for my own turn to grow.
I'm tired of feeling tired, and worried,
and secretly
scarily
furious.

That night, as I paint my face
in a snarling bear design, it feels natural
to be someone else for a change.

Gabe wears my magician's hat
with a stuffed toy rabbit
hidden inside.

Even though he can't see the toy,
Gabe knows it's there, because
his genius-nose always shows him
invisible secrets.

Gracie wears a red and gold sari
from India, and the spotted horse
is dressed as a funny elephant,
with a floppy trunk
made of braided hay
that keeps vanishing
into a horse-mouth.

I'm too shy to say it out loud
but Gracie looks pretty
and she's starting to act
as if she likes me
in a teenage way

that makes me
feel dizzy.

The cabins are too far apart
for trick-or-treating, so we play
all sorts of hilarious games
at a Cowboy Church Carnival
where Gabe and I ride perched
on top of a giant pumpkin
in a decorated wagon
pulled by Gracie's
elephant-horse.

I imagine it's the last time I'll feel
young enough to enjoy acting silly,
but it's also the first time I've ever
been old enough to laugh
at people
in monster suits.

In my other life, Halloween
meant guarding the pit bulls
from drunk, costumed thieves.

In my other life
all the monstrous nightmares
were real.

But everything isn't always
easy now. Instead, the hours flip
back and forth between hopeful
and sad.

There's an ugly surprise waiting for me
at the end of my life's first happy
Halloween. It comes in the form
of a call that makes Mom's
phone voice
sound as poisonous
as deadly nightshade berries.
Mom's in trouble. She's been fighting.
A guard was hurt. Time will be added
to her sentence. Years will be added
to my foster care.

Tío doesn't make me wonder
what will happen next.

He tells me right away
that he wants to raise me,
one way or another, either
as my foster dad—or if Mom
and the family court judge
can agree—as my really, truly
adopted dad
forever!

But it's not just him, B.B. wants me too.
When they talk about OUR family,
Tío calls her Beatrice, or Bee,
and suddenly, I realize that she
has a name of her own.
She's not just Gracie's grandma
or a bear biologist. She's herself,
helping me figure out how
to be myself.

Best of all, she'll soon be
my foster mom, or maybe even
my adopted mom,
because beautifully brave

Beatrice and my hero-uncle
are getting married!

With Gracie's parents due
to come home soon,
I won't even have to worry
about becoming anything weird
like my best friend's stepbrother.

Being part of the family seems
so complicated and exciting
that I feel like a dog
in a pack of strays,
trying to understand
glances and gestures
because I don't have
enough words
to express
my wildly
wondrously
mixed-up
feelings.

36 GABE THE DOG
WINNERS

I don't know what all
his fast human words
mean

but I love the sound of Tony's
happiest voice

so I listen
and I sniff his hands

until I'm sure his mood rhymes
with winning a shared
hide-and-seek
game.

37 TONY THE BOY
PUPPY TESTING

Gracie's parents are back just in time
for an engagement party.
Gabe and I will both be the best men
at a wedding in the spring,
but for now, I don't have to dress up.
I just wear regular clothes,
and watch grown-ups dancing
half-festive island salsa,
and half-calm, cool, old-folks
American.

Everything's changing
so fast
that I feel
like I'm sliding

down
   down
        another
steep
   mountain slope
before climbing
back uphill
one granite boulder
at a time

until I'm level and calm
instead of scrambling
and scared.

I don't know all the details
of how I'm going to feel
about losing Mom

and gaining a family
that's sort of unusual
but also pretty normal.

I do know how I feel
about Gabe—he's brave, goofy,

smart, silly, bouncy, and I love him
like a brother.

Gabe and Tío both help me enjoy
our first Thanksgiving
as a family.

With snow on the trees
that surround the corrals
of Cowboy Church, the forest
looks like it's draped in lace
or spiderwebs
or magic.

The wedding is months away,
so for now it's just me and Tío
and Gabe, and this feeling
of finally understanding
a few simple words
like safety
and hope.

At night, in the cabin,
while Gabe and I gaze

out the window at stars
I find myself wondering
if the lost-and-found hunter
will decide to stop killing
when he's not hungry,
now that he knows
how it feels to be lost
in the wild.

I hope the hound is healthy
and happy, and I hope I can really
learn math
so I can study science
in college, maybe even get into
veterinary school.
I could figure out new cures
for dog wounds, and learn how to heal
bear diseases and elephant injuries . . .
but I'll need great grades
in algebra and geometry,
all the tests of number courage
that stand between me
and my future.

I sleep with fine dreams at night—
running dreams—racing toward
something happy, instead of running
away from fangs and claws. . . .

Then, on a cold, clear morning
between Thanksgiving and Christmas,
there's another burst of amazement
in my life, an unexpected gift.
Magic, real, living, breathing
trail magic—a puppy!

Gabe is already six. He can only work
for a few more years, so Tío has decided
that I should help raise our family's
next hero, a puppy that will need
nearly two years of training
before it can rescue the lost.

Quickly, I figure out the math.
If we start teaching a puppy now,
it will be six when I reach eighteen,
the wizardly number
that will make me an adult,

allowing me to join a real search-and-rescue team.
$12+6$. It's so hard to believe.
In just $3+3$ years I'll be able
to volunteer as a SAR dog handler,
instead of a make-believe victim
who hides.

Choosing a puppy is an art.
The lowland animal shelter
is so crowded with homeless dogs
that I have to remember: looks
don't matter! Cute and cuddly
or bony and rat-haired, it's the nose
we need, along with a brave,
loyal temperament.

Sorrowful eyes. Mournful whines.
So many lonely dogs, all hoping
to be adopted! I wish we could
take them all.

We have to choose.
It's part of adult life, this constant
narrowing of wild wishes

down to one calm task
at a time.

Tío shows me how to follow
the scientific process of puppy testing.
We have to figure out which pups
are calm enough to let us teach them,
curious enough to crave work-play,
bold enough to explore,
and attentive enough to persist,
no matter how challenging
the hide-and-seek-game.

Puppy testing is the best work-fun
I've ever had in my 6 + 6 years.
At the back of my excited mind,
I'm already writing an article
for the school paper,
and a poem for my blog.
There's no rule that says
a scientist can't also
love words.

Puppy testing is simple—
I cradle each pup to see
if it's friendly and trusting.
Then, since a SAR dog can't fear
sudden movements—umbrellas,
crumpled sheets of tumbling paper,
or spooky, windblown plastic bags—
we test their courage. And we play!
We check to see which puppies
love to chase toys,
and which won't give up
in a long tug-of-war game,
but we also need a calm pup
that knows how to rest when tired,
not a nervous one that acts crazy.

We scratch bellies, pat heads,
and press down on paws with our fingers
to see how each puppy reacts
to being touched, rubbed, hugged,
and loved—a SAR dog can't be mean.
Aggressive dogs aren't allowed
to do search-and-rescue work.
Bullies aren't qualified
to be heroes.

We keep score.
We assign numbers.
Tío trusts me with the
scientific math.

The highest puppy test score
goes to a brave, focused,
curious, wolf-eyed splash
of sun-yellow fur.

She's three months old.
Her stumpy tail and yellow color
mean she's probably a mix
of supersmart Australian shepherd
and energetically friendly
golden retriever.

When we choose her, the surprise
isn't over yet—with a satisfied grin,
Tío writes my name on all
the adoption papers! I officially
have my own dog now. I'm considered
responsible. I'm practically
a grown-up.

Then comes the naming.
Short sounds, to make it easy
for the dog to learn, and maybe
a human name, to remind
everyone my puppy meets
that dogs need the same
love and care
as people.

I don't want a name that rhymes
with NO or BAD, or a confusing sound
that rhymes with any command.

I try out dozens of girls' names.
Summer? Too long. Dawn?
Not quite bright enough
for her soft golden fur.

Then it strikes me—I'm not limited
to English. Tío knows Spanish.
He can teach me. By next year's
Hispanic Heritage Month,
would I be halfway fluent?
Could I speak to my class

about learning my family's
language? Would I start
to feel like a part of two
natural places
at once?

We're still in the shelter, playing
with my newly adopted SAR pup,
when I start asking Tío to suggest
one-syllable island sounds.
He gives me Paz. Peace.
Mar, Sea.
Miel. Honey.
Luz. Light.
As soon as I hear that last one,
I know it's perfect. Luz sounds
exactly like this gold frizz of fur.
Luz and the Trail Beast.

I hope Gabe will like Luz—she's
bouncy and playful, he'll never
feel old, as long as we're all
walking
or running

or searching
together. . . .

From now on, I expect
only good dreams.

38 GABE THE DOG
FULL MOON

The yellow puppy's milky scent rhymes
with roundness, and the sound of her name
almost rhymes with moon, and when I sing, she sings,
and she understands chase games,
so we're friends, but I'm older,
so I get to teach her
all about life.

39 LUZ THE DOG FINDING HOME

In my other life there were mean kids.
I was called hey mutt, but now I'm Luz,
and I have my own boy who takes me
to puppy obedience kindergarten
at the dog-and-horse church

and who lives with me in a house
with a man and a big dog in a forest
where I sniff
sniff
    sniff
sniff
as I follow little footprint trails that always
lead me back to my boy whose scent
rhymes with home.

HOW TO STAY FOUND IN THE WONDROUS WOODS

BY GABE, LUZ, AND TONY

* Never hike alone.

* Tell someone where you're going, and how long you'll be gone.

* Stay on marked trails.

* Take plenty of water and high-energy foods.

* Make sure the adults who go with you have the right equipment (GPS, satellite phone).

* If you do get lost, remember that many plants are poisonous. Only gobble wild berries if you recognize them as familiar—blackberries,

strawberries, raspberries. Surprise: insects are some of the safest wild foods! If you're starving, try to think like a bear. They eat ant eggs, beetle grubs, grasshoppers, and crickets. (Never nibble spiders.)

🐾 If you're lost, don't panic. Stay in one place. Hug a tree. Every time you wander in circles, you make it harder for a four-footed trail angel to find you.

🐾 Trust the dog's nose.

A NOTE TO READERS

The characters in *Mountain Dog* are imaginary, but the story was inspired by a real boy, and real dogs. One of my husband's search-and-rescue dogs, Maggi, is a calm, wise Australian Shepherd/Queensland Heeler cross. Maggi came to us as a stray, needing to be rescued and adopted. She loves to herd humans, making sure we are all in one place. Our younger SAR dog, Chance, is an energetic Yellow Labrador Retriever who shares Gabe's enthusiasm for all things round and high-flying, even the moon.

When my husband trains Maggi and Chance, I serve as a volunteer "victim," hiding in the forest so the dogs can practice finding a lost person. Sometimes I just hide for a few minutes, but there are days when I have to wait for hours before a dog's smart nose finds my invisible scent trail. It feels like magic, but my husband calls it science.

Many other aspects of *Mountain Dog* were also inspired

by my real life. I have relatives who left our ancestral island on a raft. I've stood face-to-face with a bear on a trail, and I've heard a mountain lion's eerie cry. I've visited a sad, confused woman in prison. I've seen mountain areas remote enough to have tiny, old-fashioned schools, as well as cowboy churches where horses and dogs are welcome. I used to dread math, but in order to study botany and agriculture, I had to overcome my fear of numbers.

Most of all, throughout my life, whether on wilderness paths or city sidewalks, I have often received trail magic in the form of unexpected acts of kindness from strangers.

I hope you enjoy reading *Mountain Dog* as much as I enjoyed writing it!

YOUR FRIEND,

MARGARITA ENGLE
CLOVIS, CALIFORNIA

ACKNOWLEDGMENTS

I thank God for wilderness and trail angels.

I am joyfully grateful to Curtis, our dogs, the rest of our family, and the following canine search-and-rescue organizations: CARDA, MADSAR, SLOSAR, and NSDA. Special thanks to Kai Hernández, Norma Snelling, Nancy Acebo, and Dr. Cheryl Waterhouse.

I wish to express profound gratitude to Ann Martin and Laura Godwin for this opportunity to write about canine trail magic. Special thanks to Kate Butler, April Ward, and the entire Holt/Macmillan publishing team.

I am grateful to Olga and Alexey Ivanov for their beautiful illustrations.

Go Fish!

GO FISH

MARGARITA ENGLE

What did you want to be when you grew up?
I wanted to be a wild horse.

When did you realize you wanted to be a writer?
As a child, I wrote poetry. Stories came much later. I always loved to read, and I think that for me, longing to write was just the natural outgrowth of loving to read.

What's your first childhood memory?
When I was two, a monkey pulled my hair at the Havana Zoo. I remember my surprise quite vividly.

What's your most embarrassing childhood memory?
When I was very little, we lived in a forest. I wandered around a hunter's cabin, and found a loaded gun behind a door. I remember feeling so terribly ashamed when people yelled at me for pointing the gun at them. I had no idea I was doing anything wrong.

What's your favorite childhood memory?
Riding horses on my great-uncle's farm in Cuba.

As a young person, who did you look up to most?
Growing up in Los Angeles, I participated in civil rights marches. I admired Martin Luther King Jr. I was also a great fan of Margaret Mead. I wanted to travel all over the world, and understand the differences and similarities between various cultures.

What was your worst subject in school?
Math and PE. I was a klutz in every sport, and I needed a tutor to get through seventh-grade algebra. In high school, my geometry teacher crumpled my homework, threw it on the floor, stepped on it, and said, "This is trash!"

What was your best subject in school?
English. I loved reading, and I loved writing term papers.

What was your first job?
Cleaning houses.

How did you celebrate publishing your first book?
Disbelief, and then scribbling some more.

Where do you write your books?
I do a lot of my writing outdoors, especially in nice weather.

Where do you find inspiration for your writing?
Old, dusty, moldy, tattered, insect-nibbled history books, and the stories my mother and grandmother used to tell me about our family.

Which of your characters is most like you?
I'm not nearly as brave as any of my characters.

Did you have a dog growing up?
I grew up in the big city of Los Angeles, but my sister and I were fortunate to have parents who allowed us to have pets of all sorts. We adopted stray dogs and cats, and we nursed injured birds. Our room was filled with caterpillars turning into butterflies and tadpoles transforming into frogs. A lizard lived behind my mirror, and I had a rabbit in the garden. Sadly, my childhood dogs were not loyal. They came and went as they pleased, sometimes living with us but often going off to explore. Now, as an adult, I love having well-trained dogs that stay with us, both indoors and when we're outside, enjoying adventures.

Have you ever been lost?
I've lost my way in the wilderness. It's terrifying. All the trees start to look alike. It's natural to start running in circles, but that makes a hiker's sense of direction even less dependable. Fortunately, I found my way back to the trail and did not have to be rescued.

SQUARE FISH

When did you first get interested in search and rescue?

My husband and his SAR dogs introduced me to this amazing subject when he decided to join a volunteer search-and-rescue group shortly after September 11, 2001. Watching urban search dogs in action inspired both of us.

What sparked your imagination for *Mountain Dog*?

My husband is a volunteer wilderness search-and-rescue K-9 handler. His dogs, Maggi and Chance, need practice finding lost people, so I hide in the woods, and they find me. Hiding is relaxing for me and exciting for the dogs. It's like a game of wilderness hide-and-seek, but when someone is actually lost, all that fun becomes serious work. The incident that really made me want to write about search-and-rescue dogs was an encounter with three lost girls who cried, and told their story to Chance instead of talking to people. It helped me realize how easily children can wander away from a campground or hiking trail, and also how comforting it can be to communicate with a dog. So, first I wrote *When You Wander,* a picture book for younger children. This was followed by "Trail Magic," a short story in *Because of Shoe*, a wonderful collection of dog stories edited by Ann Martin, the fantastic author of *Everything for a Dog*. Imagine the thrill when Ann Martin asked me to expand "Trail Magic" into a full-length novel—and offered to edit it herself!

Do you have a favorite search-and-rescue story?
A few years ago there was a little girl, the daughter of farm workers, who lived near a vineyard. She wandered away from home with her dog and fell asleep under a grapevine. When search-and-rescue volunteers found her, she was curled up with her puppy, who must have been great comfort as well as protection. When I decided to include that story in *Mountain Dog*, I changed the vineyard to an apple orchard, but basically all the search stories in *Mountain Dog* are inspired by real incidents. I wanted that aspect to be authentic, not imaginary.

What advice would you give to someone who is lost?
The most important thing is to stay in one place so that searchers can find you. The farther you wander, the harder it is for a dog's smart nose to follow your scent trail. Even better, follow the basic rules for enjoying nature: never hike alone and always tell someone where you're going. That way you can have fun while staying safe!

Are you a morning person or a night owl?
Morning. By noon, I am just a phantom of my morning self, and by evening, I turn into a sponge—all I can do is read, not write.

What's your idea of the best meal ever?
A Cuban guateque. It's a country feast on a farm. It comes with music, jokes, storytelling, and impromptu poetry recitals by weathered farmers with poetic souls.

Which do you like better: cats or dogs?
I love to walk, so definitely dogs. We always have at least one cat, but cats don't like to go places. Dogs are much more adventurous.

What do you value most in your friends?
Honesty and kindness.

Where do you go for peace and quiet?
A pecan grove behind our house at least twice a day, and the Sierra Nevada Mountains, at least twice a week. When I really need tranquility, I visit giant sequoia trees. Their size, age, and beauty help me replace anxieties with amazement.

What makes you laugh out loud?
Funny poems. The sillier, the better.

What's your favorite song?
I love the rhythms and melodies of old Cuban country music, but my favorite lyrics are from a reggae song by Johnny Nash, "I Can See Clearly Now."

Who is your favorite fictional character?
That changes constantly. In other words, the one I am reading about at the moment.

What are you most afraid of?
Tidal waves, nightmares, and insomnia.

What time of year do you like best?
Spring.

What's your favorite TV show?
So You Think You Can Dance.

If you were stranded on a desert island, who would you want for company?
My husband.

If you could travel in time, where would you go?
My grandmother's childhood.

What's the best advice you have ever received about writing?
Don't worry about getting published. Just write for yourself.

What would you do if you ever stopped writing?
Read.

What do you like best about yourself?
Hope.

What is your worst habit?
Self-criticism. Talking mean to myself. I can be very discouraging.

What do you consider to be your greatest accomplishment?
Finding the poetry in history.

SQUARE FISH

Where in the world do you feel most at home?
Forests and libraries.

What do you wish you could do better?
Don't worry, be happy.

GOFISH

OLGA & ALEKSEY IVANOV

What did you want to be when you grew up?
Olga: I badly wanted to be a zoo technician and feed the big animals.
Aleksey: I always wanted to be a visual artist.

When did you realize you wanted to be an illustrator?
O: When I was in fifth grade.
A: After I graduated from art school.

What's your favorite childhood memory?
O: Picking wild mushrooms in the forest with my grandpa.
A: Gardening strawberries and building a tree house with my grandpa.

As a young person, who did you look up to most?
O: My art school teacher.
A: Michelangelo was/is my hero.

SQUARE FISH

What was your first job, and what was your "worst" job?

O: My first job was as an art teacher. My worst job was when I was commissioned to paint the portrait of a nine-month-old baby—from a live model.

A: My first job was as an artist, and it is still. I can't think of a "worst" job.

How did you celebrate publishing your first book?

O: I spent all the money I made on watercolors, paper, and brushes.

A: It was very long ago. Olga and I had a new baby by then, and there was no time for celebration.

Where do you work on your illustrations?

O: In our studio with a mountain view.

A: Olga and I are very lucky to have a studio in the house where we live and work.

Where do you find inspiration for your illustrations?

O: Everywhere.

A: All I need is to close my eyes.

What was your experience like working on *Mountain Dog*?

O: It was the perfect project for us! Aleksey and I live in the mountains and felt the story inside out. We *love* dogs.

A: It was a very interesting, easygoing project. The story hooked me right away.

Have you ever met a search-and-rescue dog?
O: Yes, they are around.
A: A few times.

Do you have any pets?
O: We have a big fluffy Samoyed called Balto.
A: I'm a dog person.

Where do you go for peace and quiet?
O: It is very peaceful and quiet where we live and illustrate. That's why we like living in the Rocky Mountains.
A: The mountains.

What are you most afraid of?
O: Flying champagne corks.
A: Scorpions and some spiders look pretty scary sometimes.

If you could travel in time, where would you go and what would you do?
O: Italy, during the Renaissance. I would go to Leonardo da Vinci's studio and ask to be his student.
A: I would also go to Italy during the Renaissance.

What's the best advice you have ever received about illustrating?
O: When I was four years old, I was trying to copy an image of a kitty and it wasn't working. My mom said, "Never give up!"
A: My teacher said, "Try it one hundred times. It'll be easy then."

What would you do if you ever stopped illustrating?
O: I hope that'll never happen.
A: I hope it will never happen.

Did you have any strange or funny habits when you were a kid?
O: When I was a kid, I liked to "fix" some illustrations in books that I thought were bad.
A: Playing "dragon" at six in the morning with my dog.

What do you consider to be your greatest accomplishment?
O: Our son.
A: To raise an artistic son.

What do you wish you could do better?
O: Skate.
A: It's all good.

What is your favorite medium to work in?
O: Watercolor and pencils.
A: Watercolor and ink.

What was your favorite book or comic/graphic novel when you were a kid?
O: Hans Christian Andersen's fairy tales.
A: *Spider-Man*.

SQUARE FISH

What challenges do you face in the artistic process, and how do you overcome them?

O: Time restrictions are very hard when you want quality, so I illustrate seven days per week.

A: I do know a magic word for situations like this. It really works.

What would your readers be most surprised to learn about you?

O: I collect shapes of ears. Every time I meet a person, I memorize his or her ear shape and then draw it in my notebook from memory.

A: My eyes work as an X-ray. I can see all of your bones, your ribs, your skull, and such. ☺ I was pretty good at anatomy lessons in art school.

SQUARE FISH